This Construction Site sticker activity book belongs to:

....

D1378816

There's a lot to do on a construction site! Can you find the right equipment on the sticker pages to add into the scene so that work can start?

Cranes are used to lift really heavy objects. Draw a heavy object for this crane to lift.

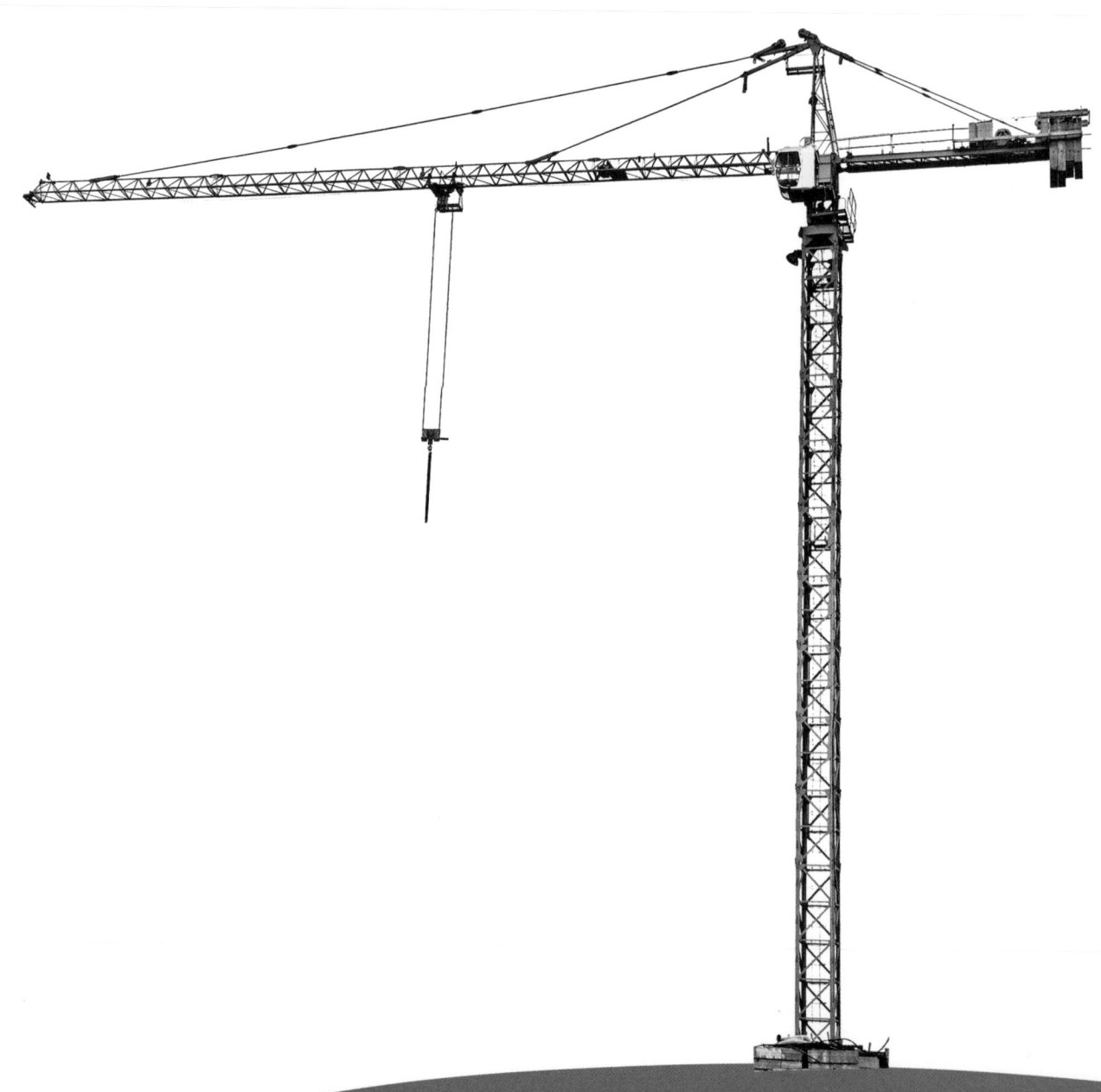

Can you find the truck that looks different from the others?

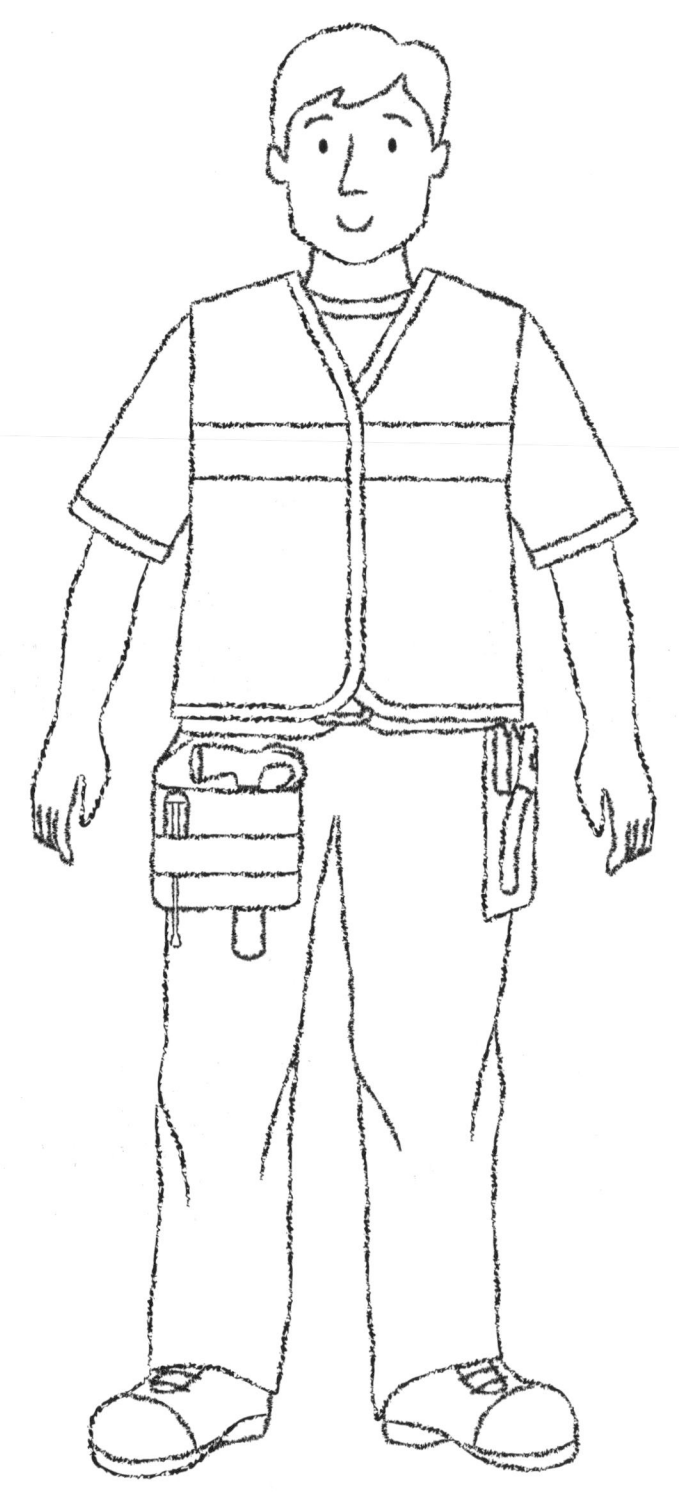

Safety is really important! Can you draw a hard hat, safety glasses, and some work gloves on this construction worker and color him in?

Color in this digging scene.

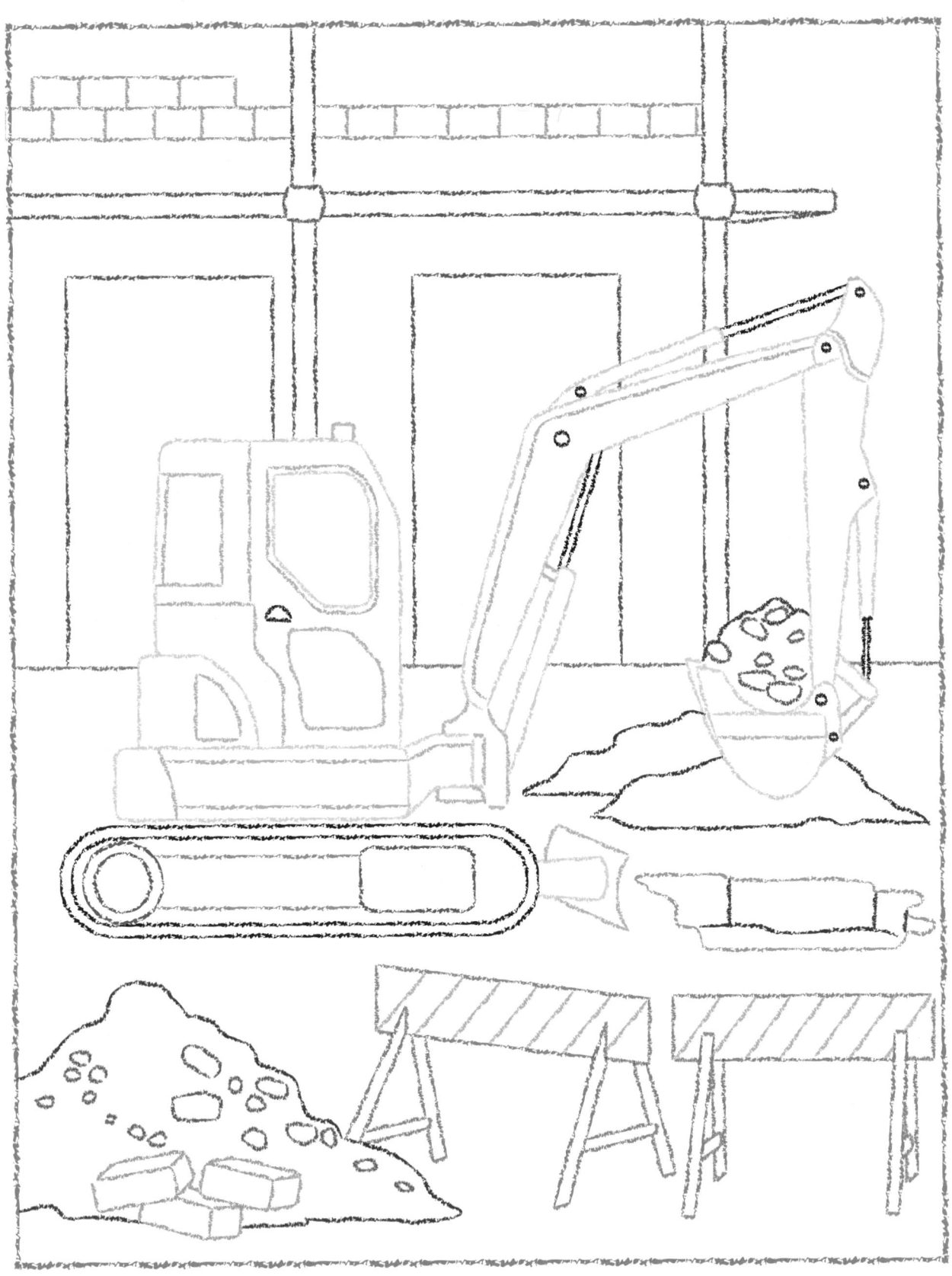

There are many different construction workers. Can you find the right tool on the sticker pages for each of the workers below?

painter

paintbrush and paint

wire

saw and wood

carpenter

electrician

bricklayer

bricks and trowel

building plans

architect

plumber

pipe wrenches
and plunger

A roofer is stuck on the roof!

Help him find his way down safely using the ladders.

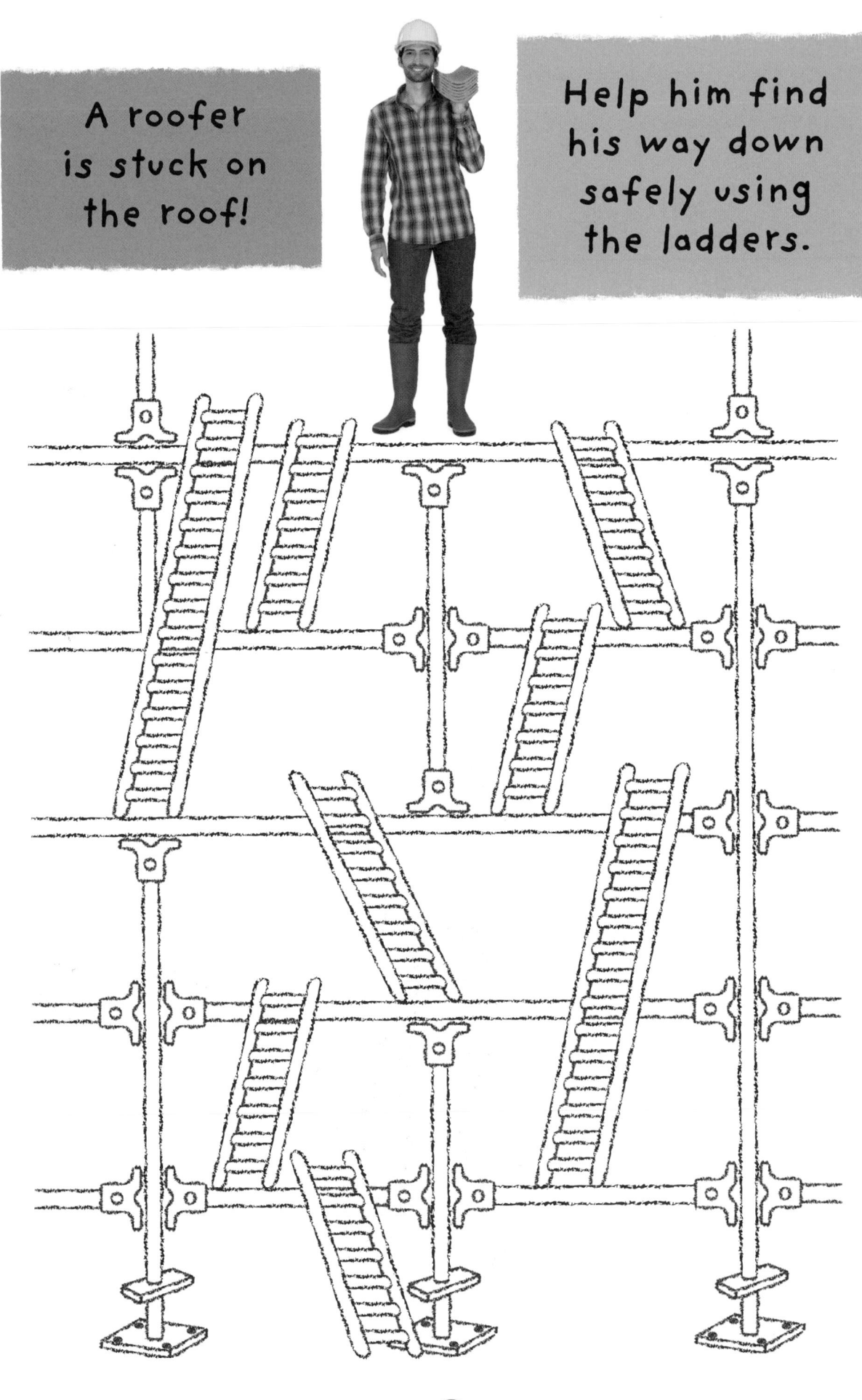

Find the 5 differences between these diggers and then color them in.

Follow the lines to see which crane is working on which building.

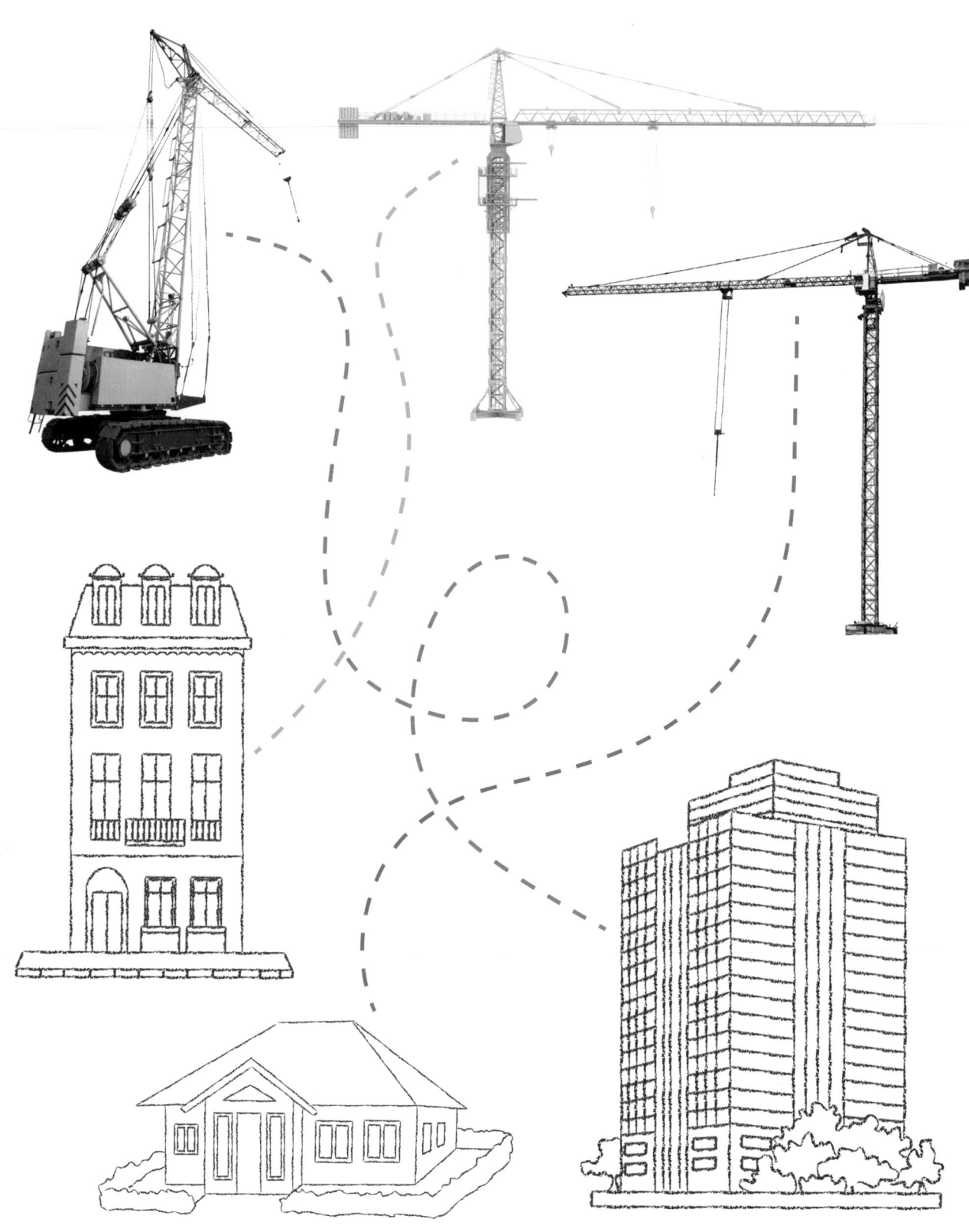

Find two steamrollers that are the same and circle them.

These construction vehicles are all missing something! Find the parts on the sticker pages to get these vehicles up and running.

The painter needs an assistant!
Brighten up this room by drawing
a pattern on the wall, and don't
forget to color it in!

Follow the lines to see which machine has moved the most earth.

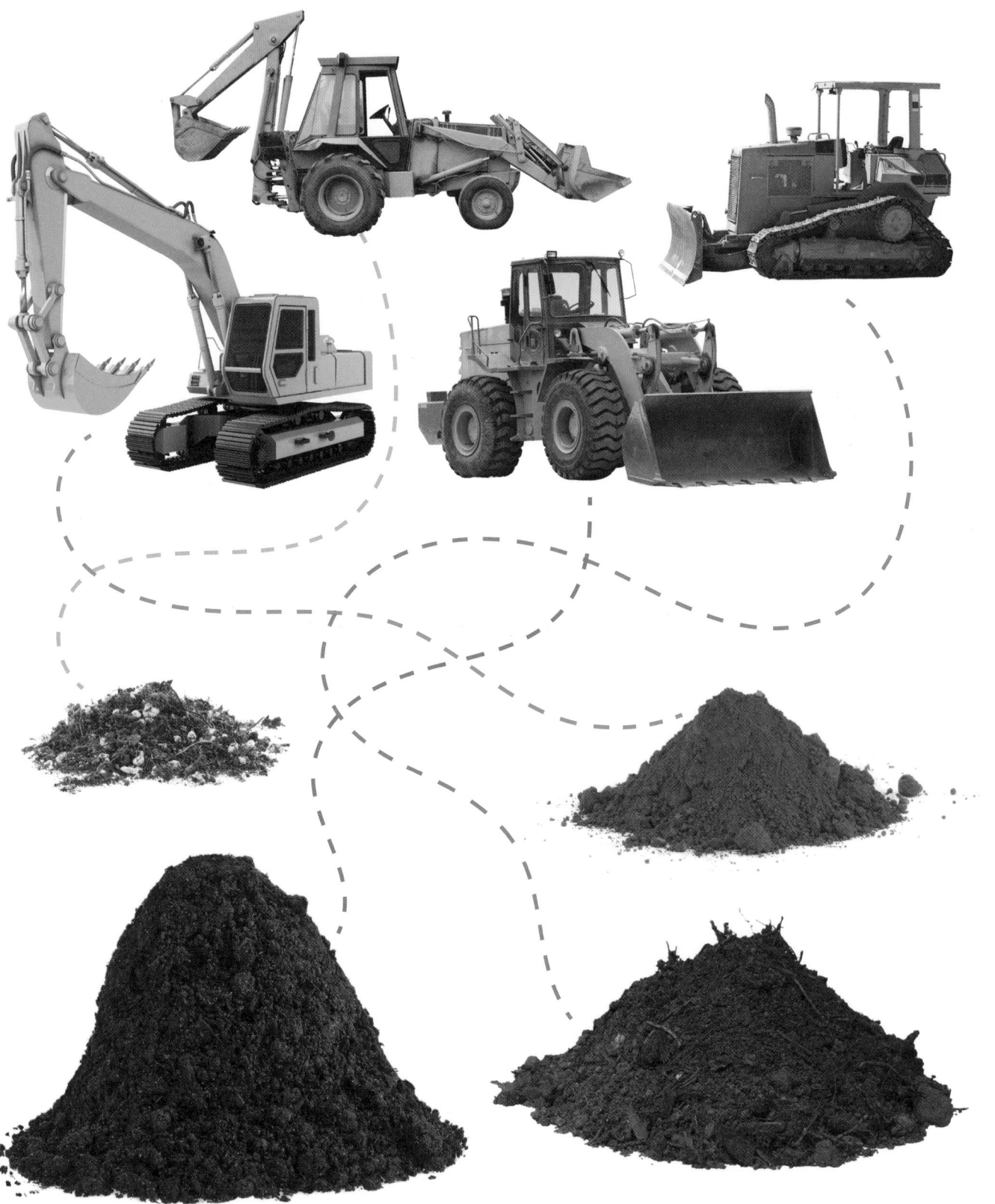

This construction worker's tool belt is empty! Can you find all of the tools on the sticker pages?

screwdriver

wrench

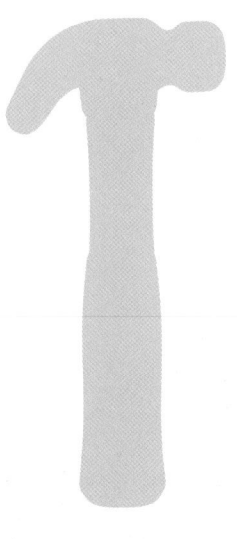

hammer

tape measure

electric drill

Oh, no! Part of this wall has crumbled! Draw some bricks to help put it back together again before it collapses.

Fill in the missing stickers. Then draw lines between the tool and the material it works with.

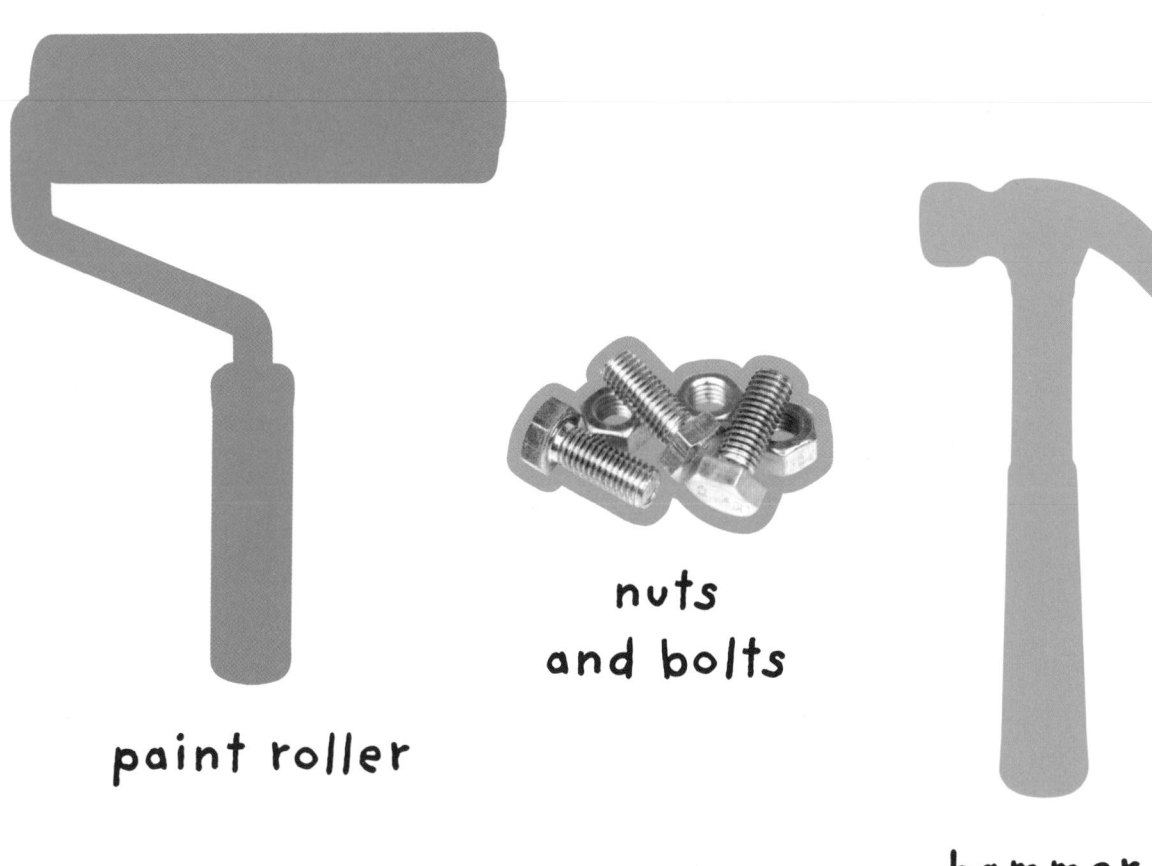

paint roller

nuts and bolts

hammer

nails

cement powder

screwdriver

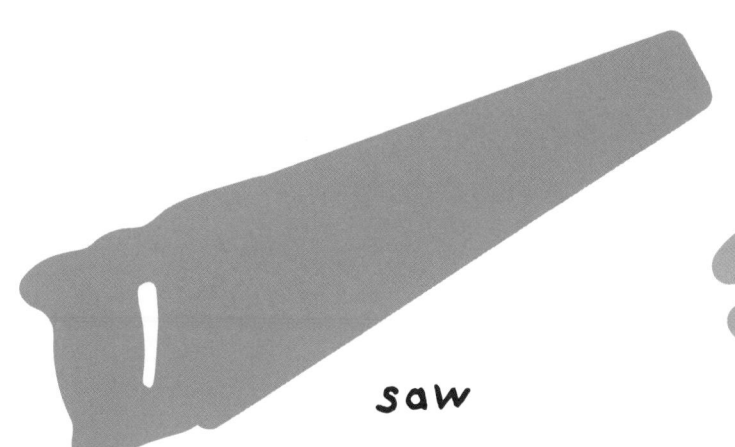

saw

wrench

cement mixer

paint

wood

screws

Can you help the forklift find the quickest way to the pallets?

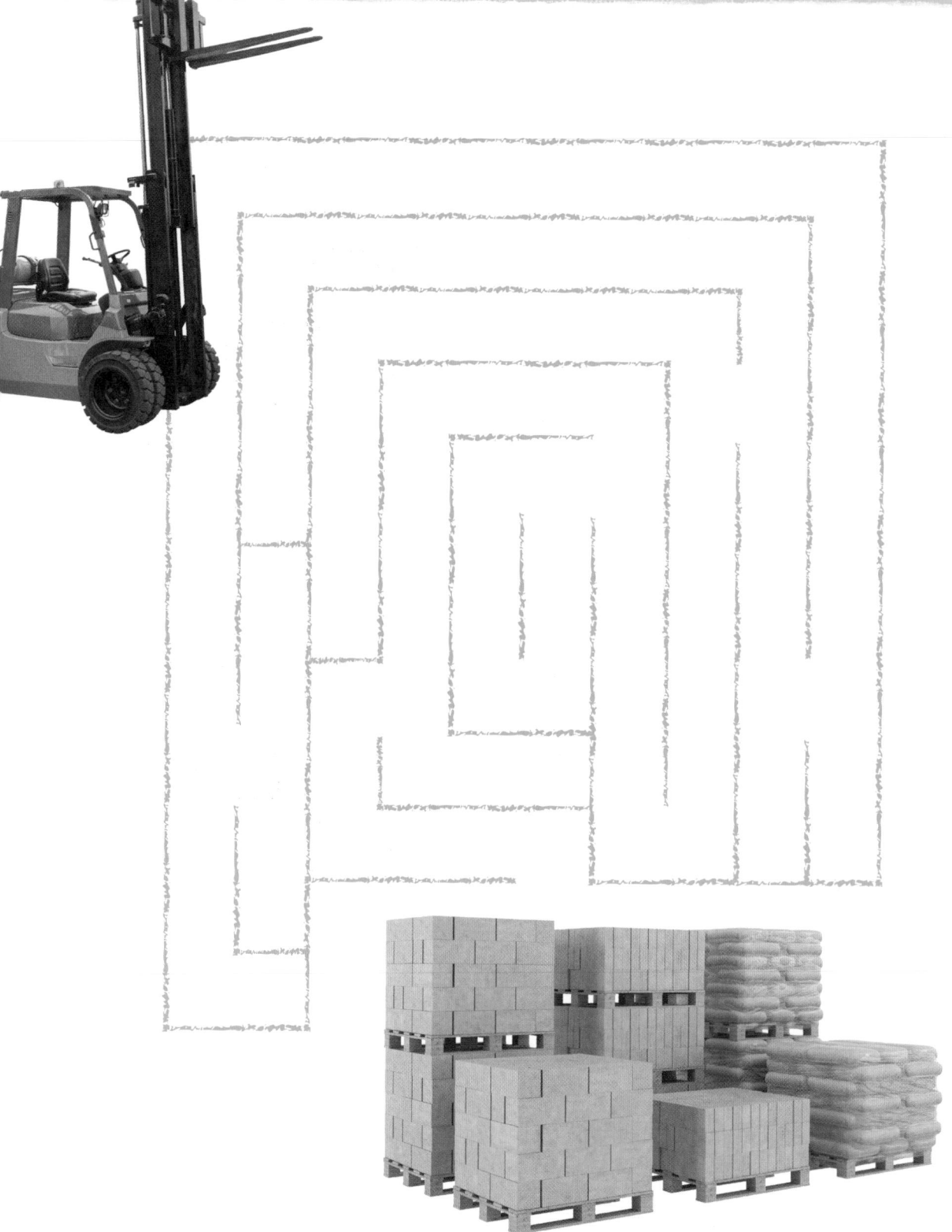

The plumber needs some help!
Find the pipe stickers to connect
the sink to the water tank.

Follow the lines to complete the drawing of this crane and wrecking ball. Now color in the scene.

A carpenter makes things out of wood. Can you find her missing tools on the sticker pages?

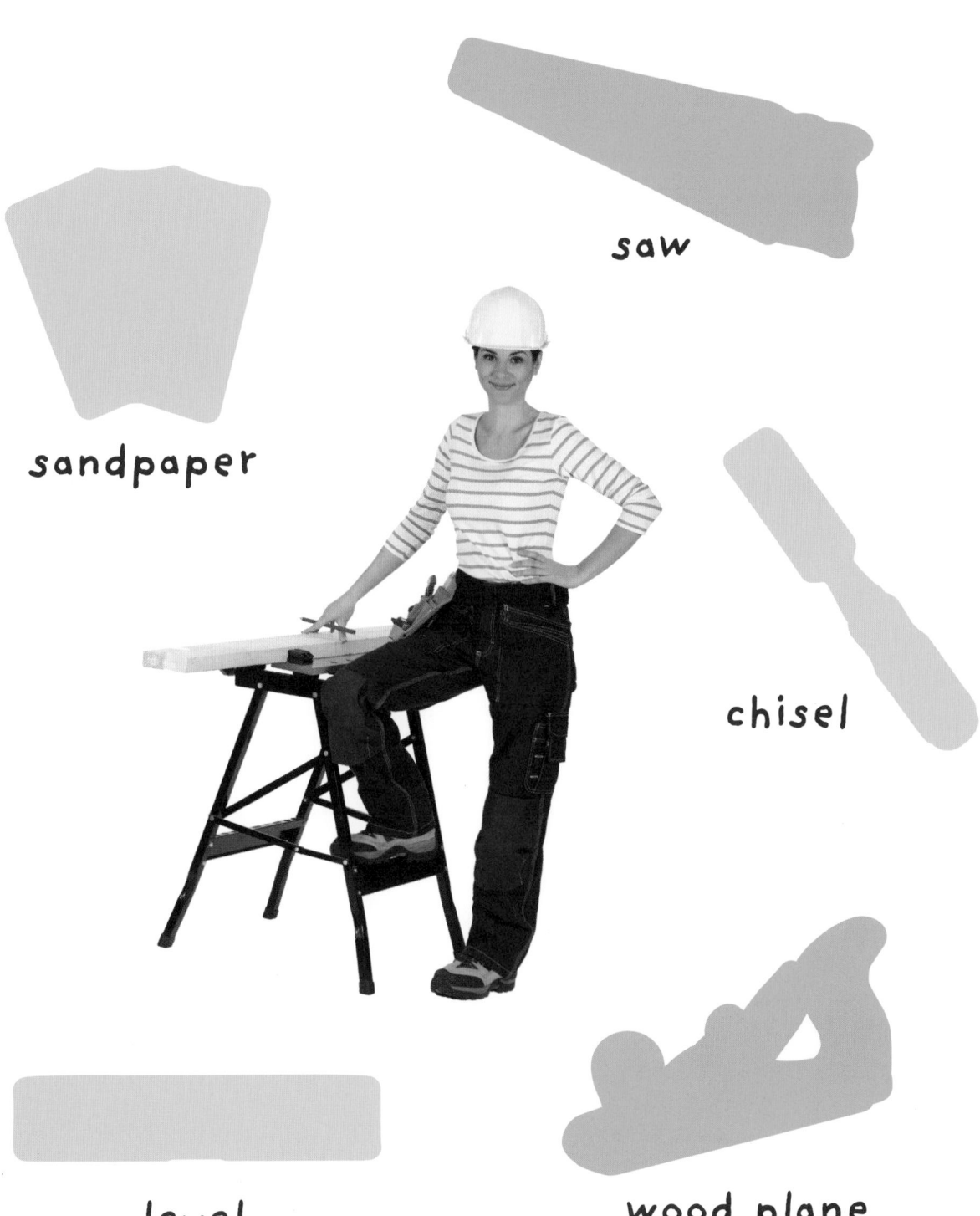

saw

sandpaper

chisel

level

wood plane

These trucks have very important materials to deliver. Can you match the right truck to the right construction site?

Can you find the pile of bricks that looks different from the others?

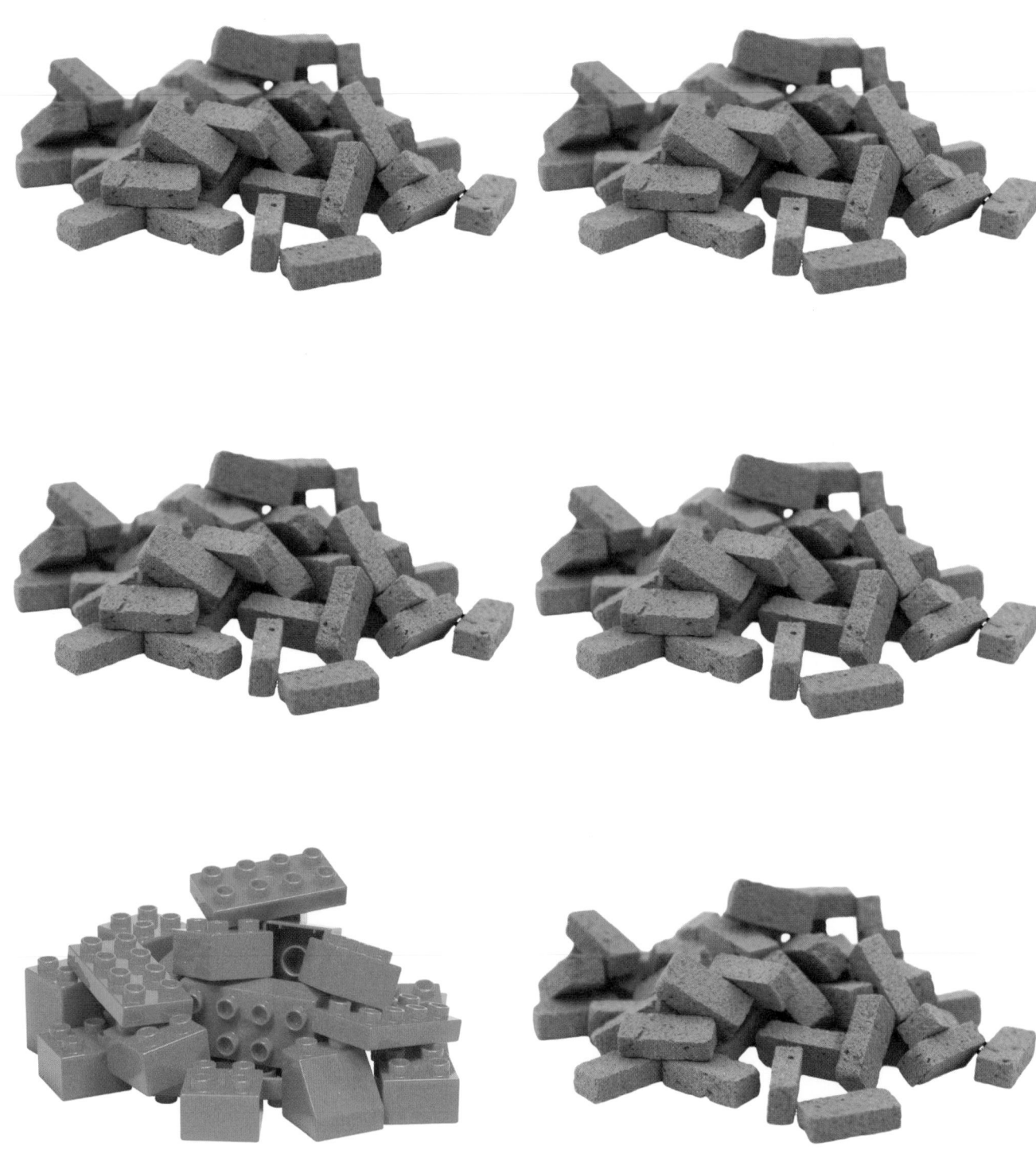

Find the toolboxes on the sticker pages, and then follow the lines to see which toolbox belongs to which construction worker.

Complete the unfinished skyscrapers by adding windows. Then color in the scene.

Circle the five items that help protect workers on the construction site.

Which tracks belong to which vehicle? Match each construction vehicle to the tracks they are most likely to make.

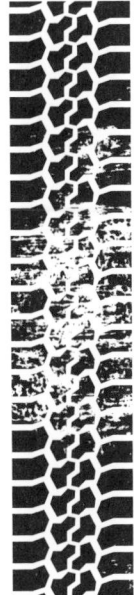
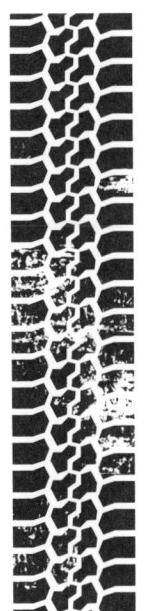

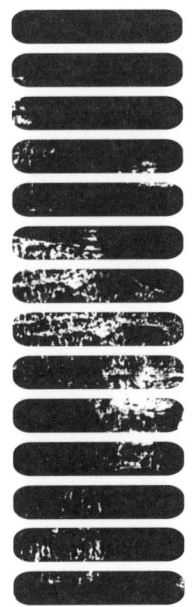

Find the 6 differences between these construction workers and then color them in.

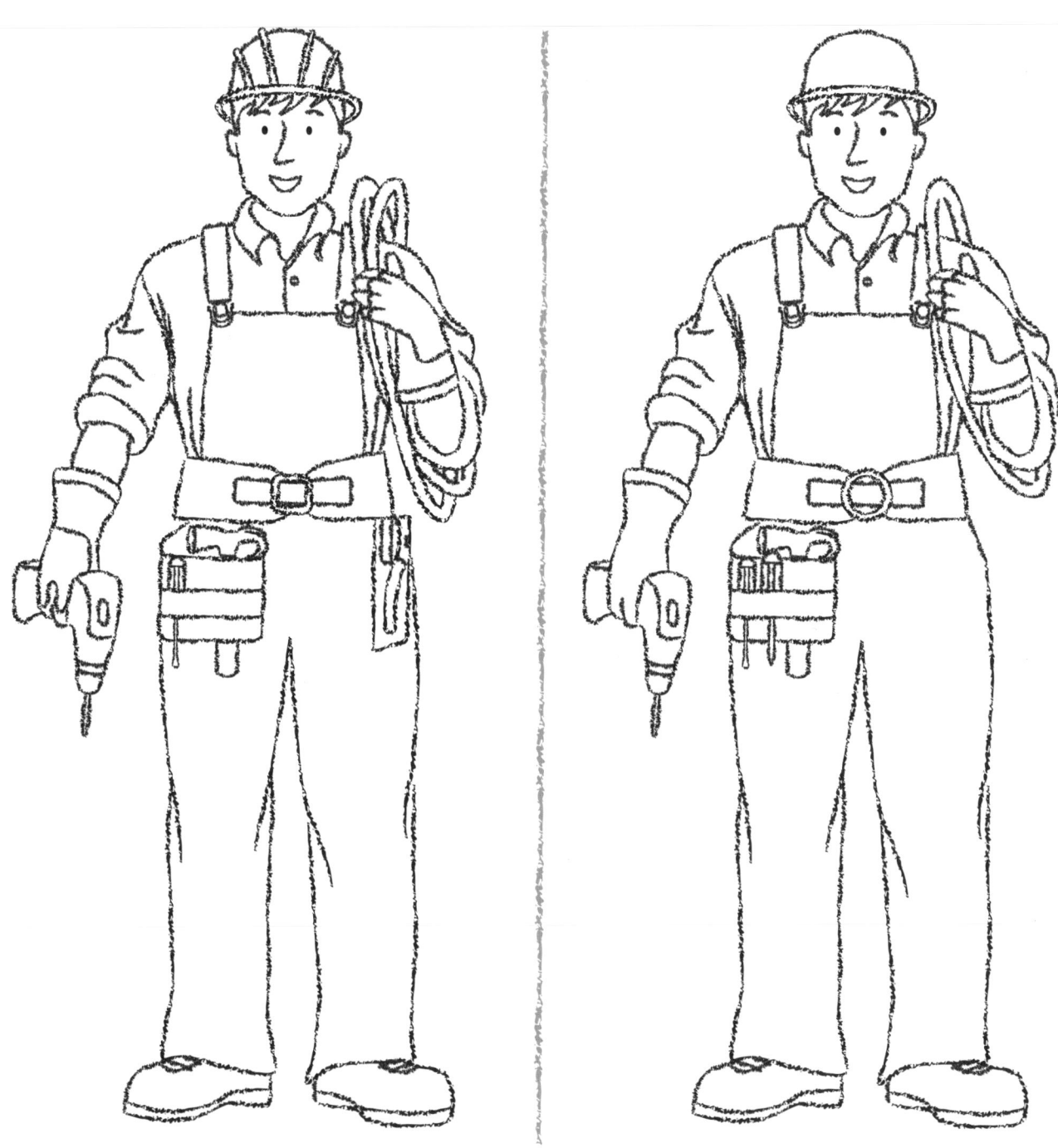

Find the chimney and tile pieces on the sticker pages to complete this roof.

Buildings are made using strong materials to keep them standing tall. Circle all the construction materials on this page.

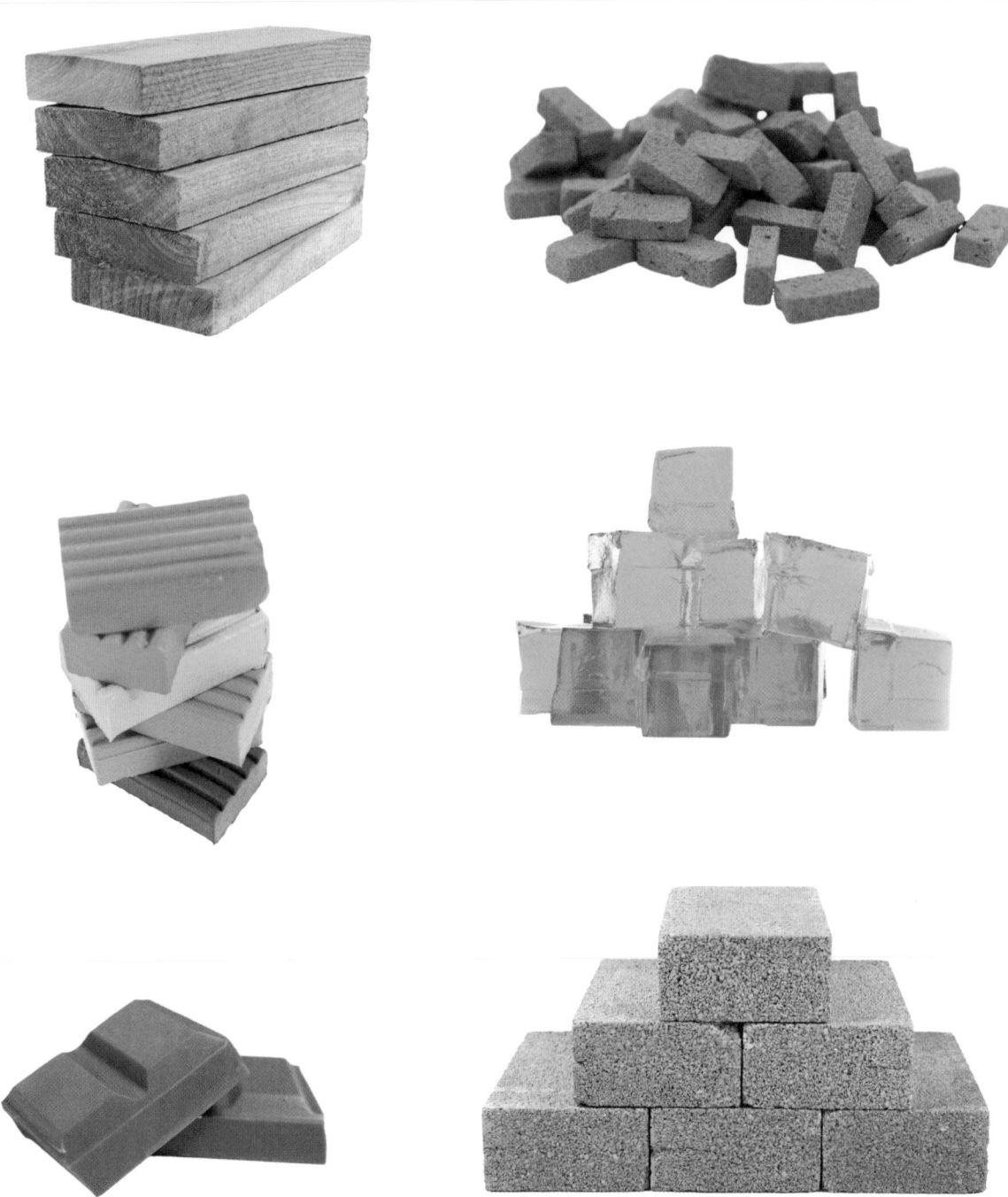

An electrician connects all the wires to the main power supply. Can you find his missing tools on the sticker pages?

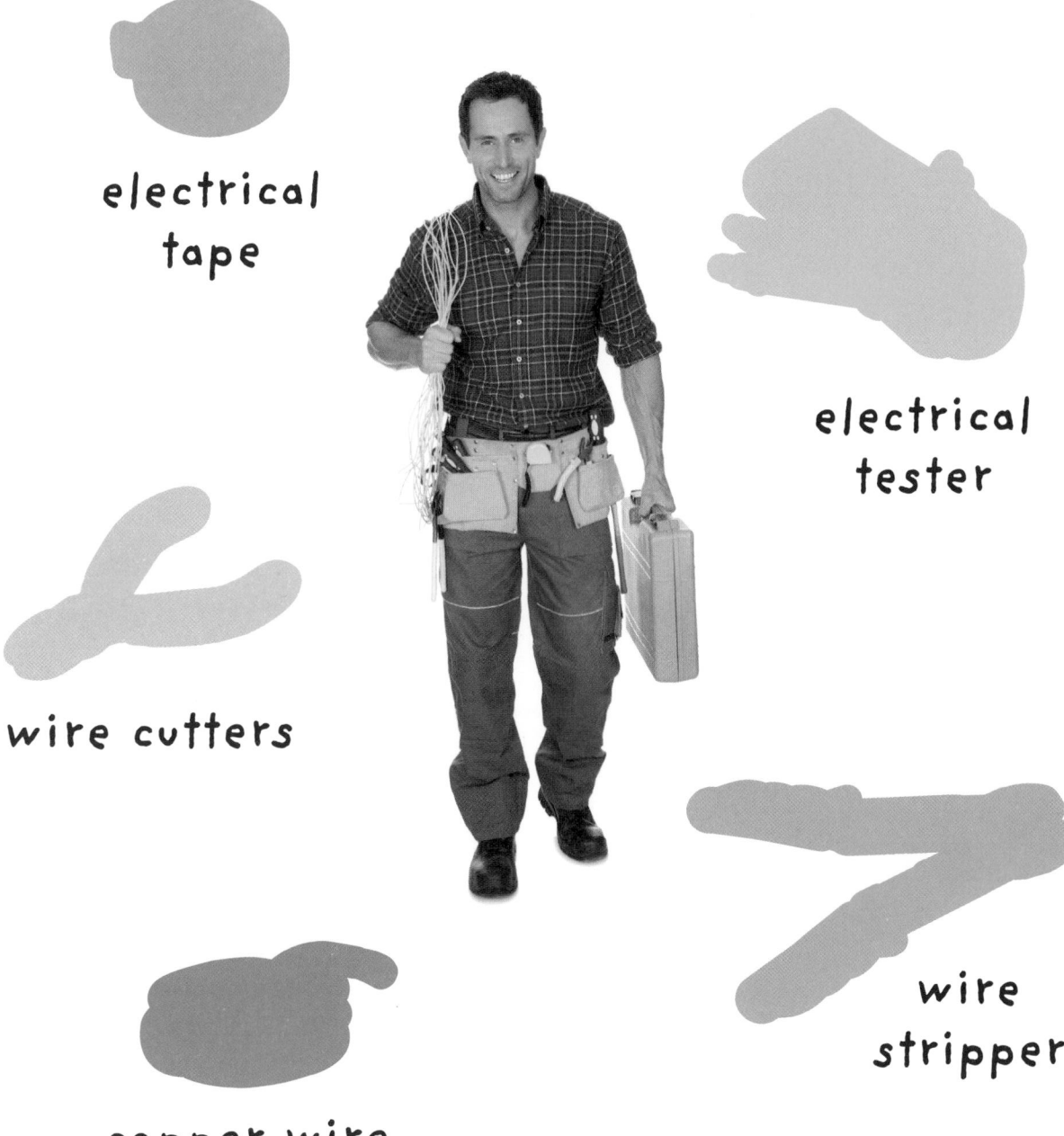

electrical tape

electrical tester

wire cutters

wire stripper

copper wire

There are eight things in this scene that don't belong on a construction site. Can you find them all?

Oh, no! This construction worker has overslept! Help him find the quickest way to the construction site.

Can you find the object that looks different from the others?

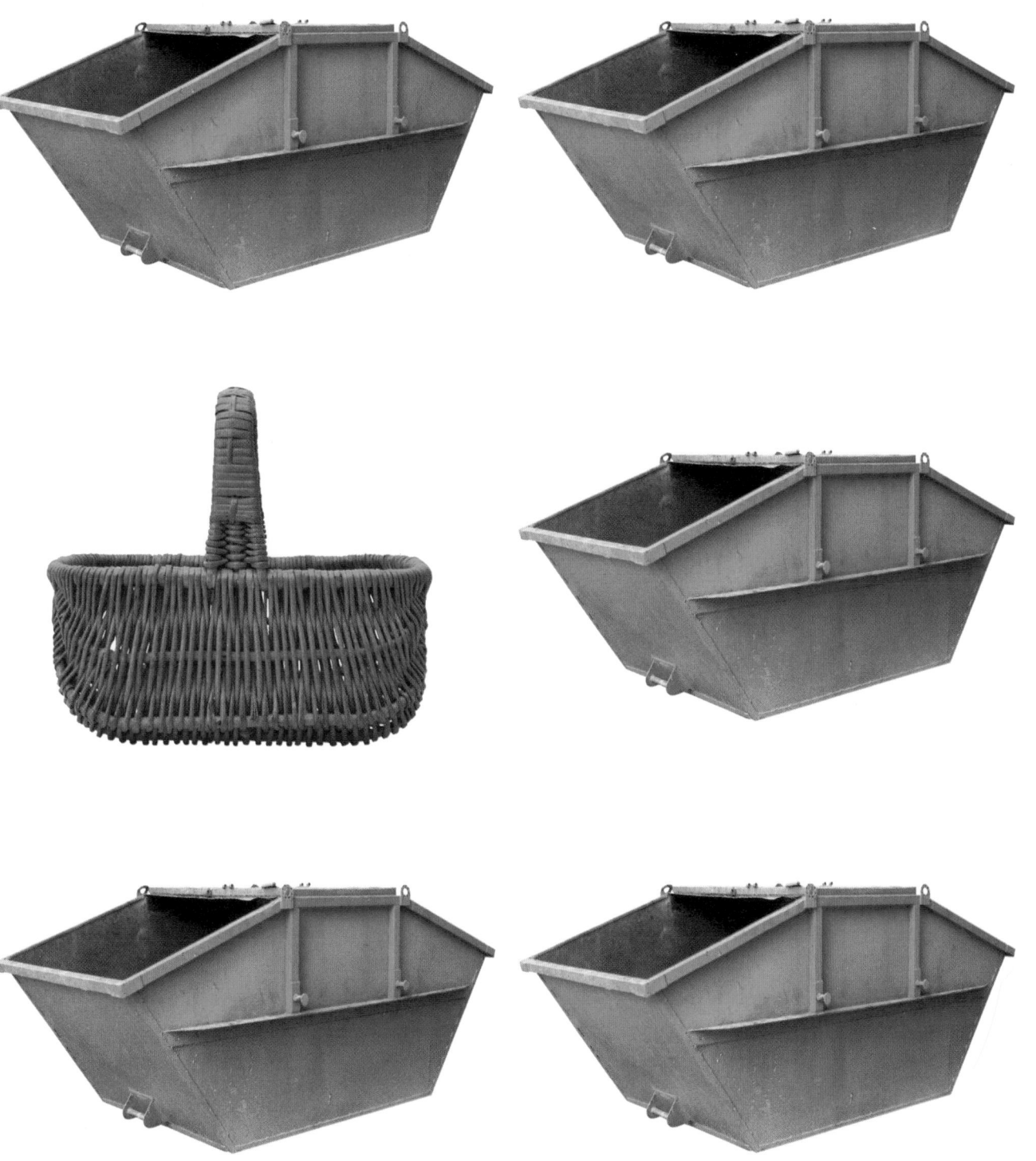

Find the two identical construction workers and circle them.

Architects design buildings. Connect the dots to see what building this architect is designing next.

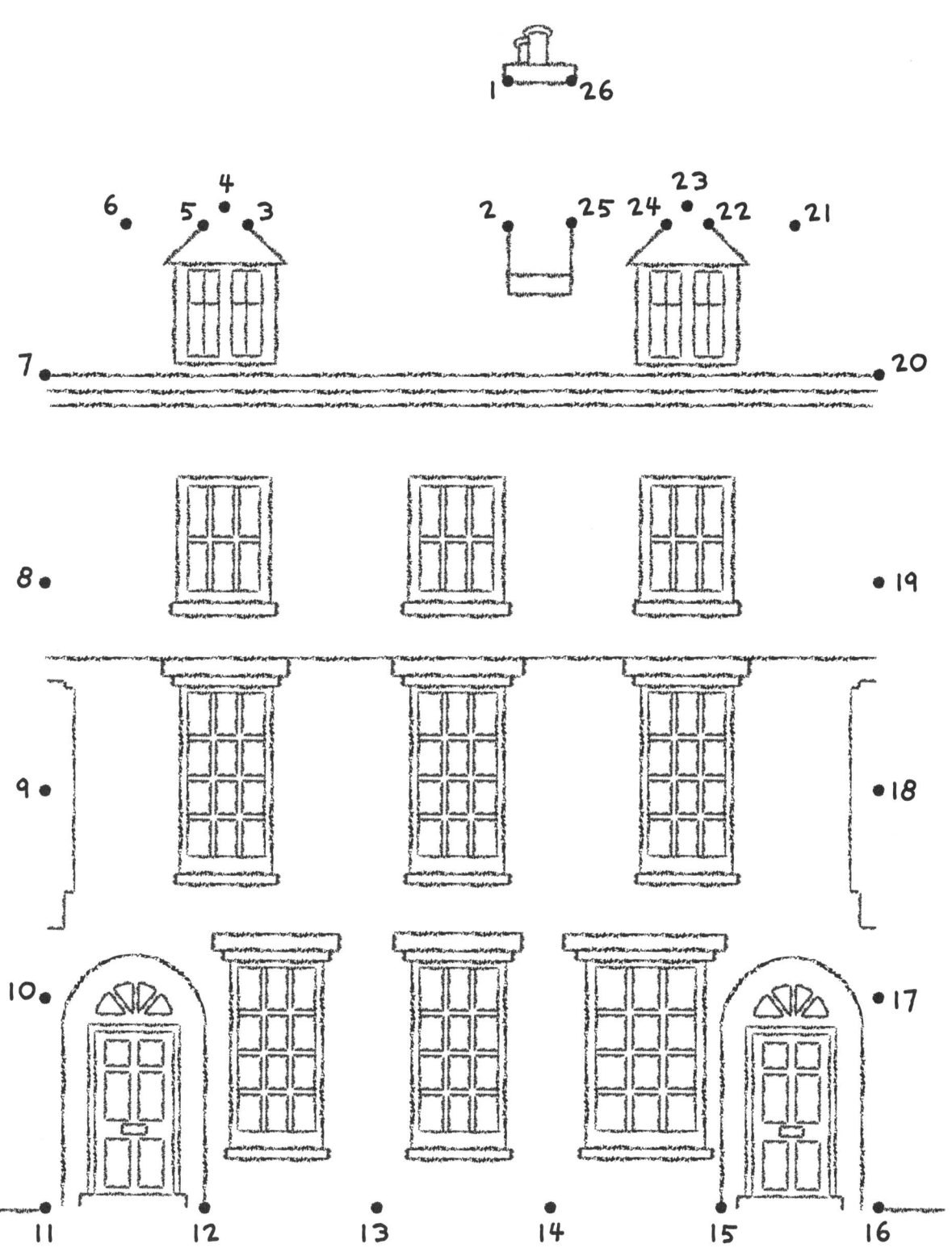

Find 10 differences between these two building sites, and then color in the pictures!

Six tools have been hidden in
the brick wall. Can you find
and name them all?

A plumber connects pipes to the main water supply. Can you find her missing tools on the sticker pages?

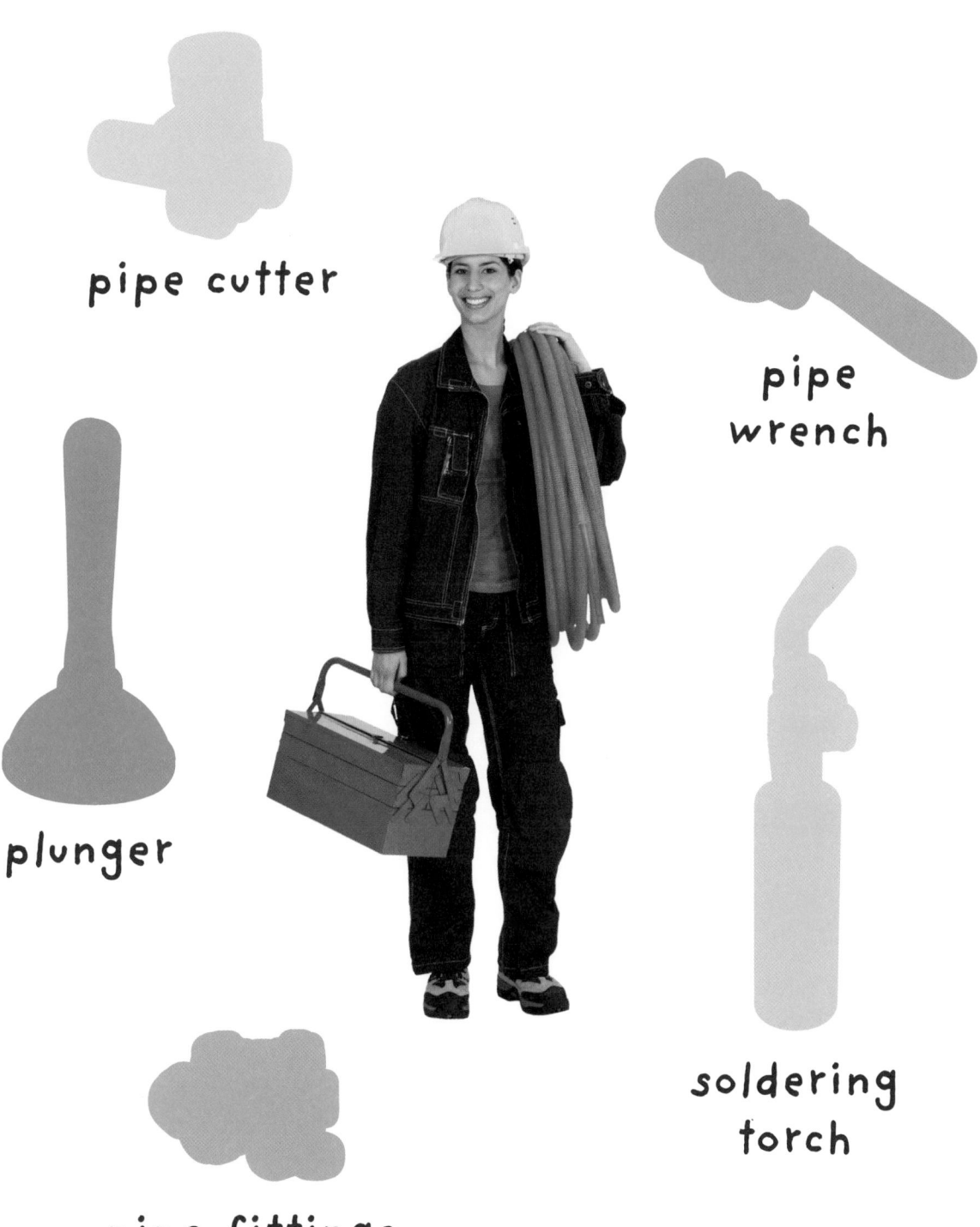

pipe cutter

pipe wrench

plunger

soldering torch

pipe fittings

Follow the lines to complete these construction vehicles and then color them in!

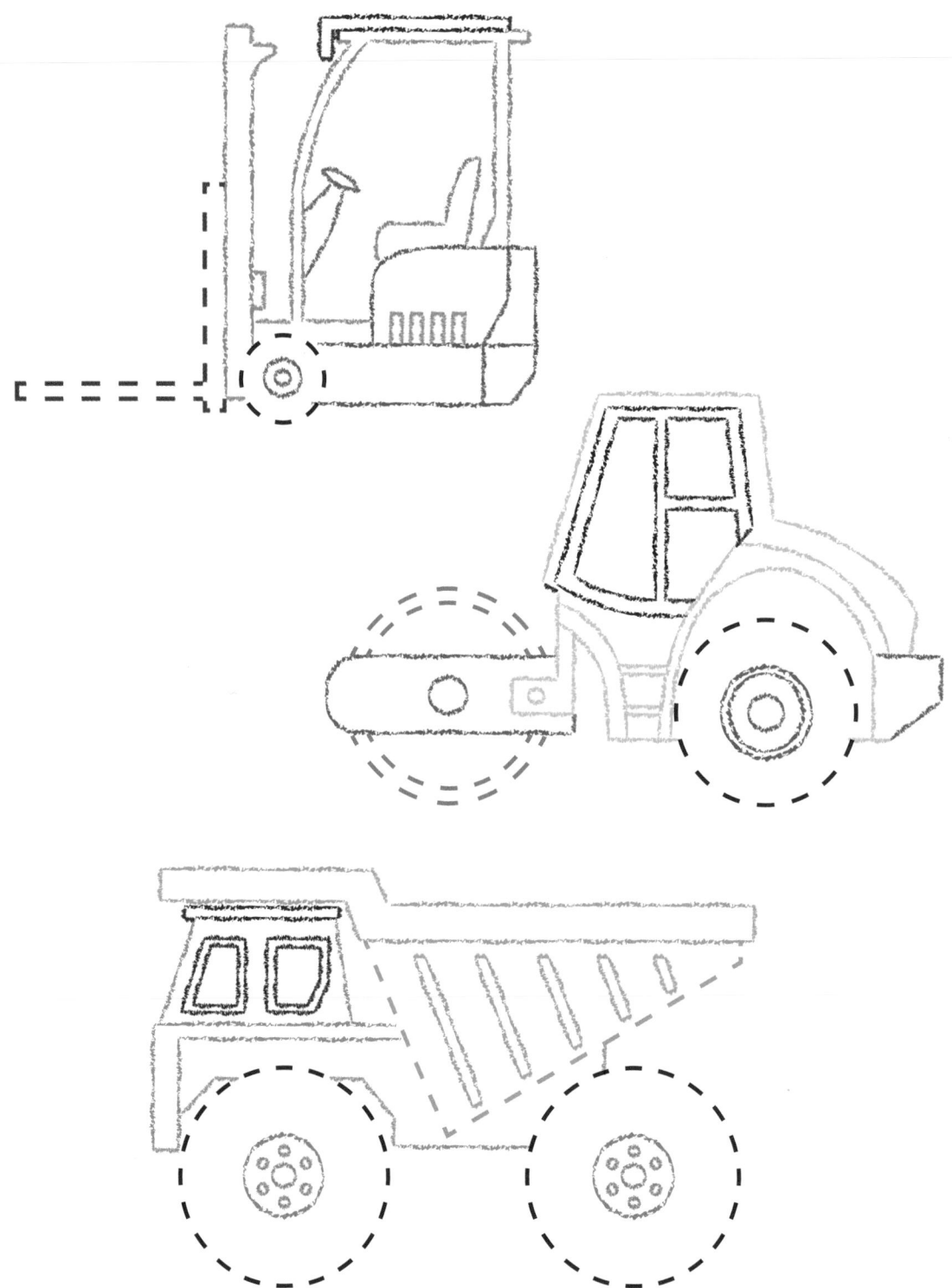

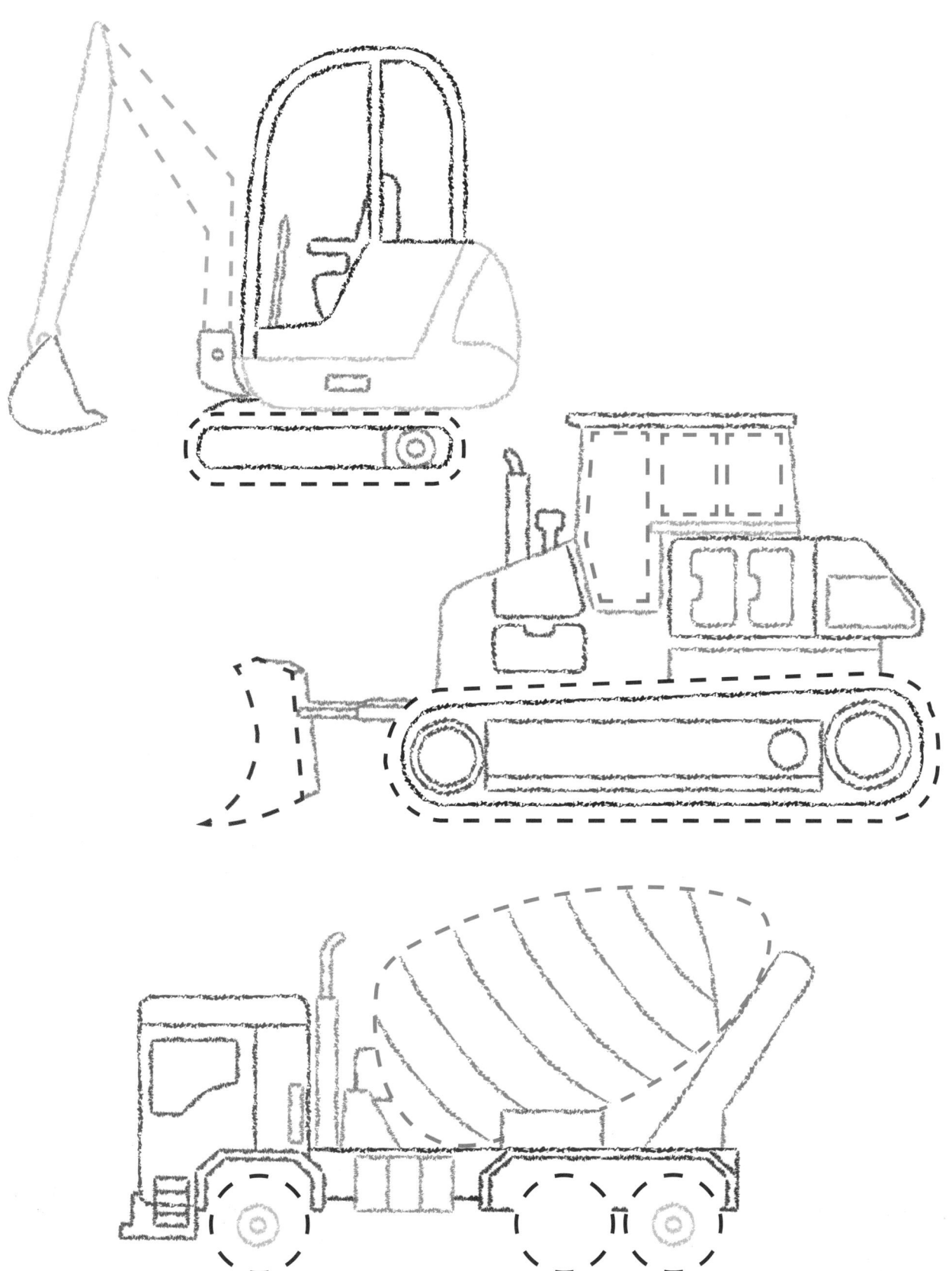

Find the two
dump trucks that
are the same and
circle them.

Draw in the wheels to help this steamroller flatten the uneven road. Don't forget to color in the scene.

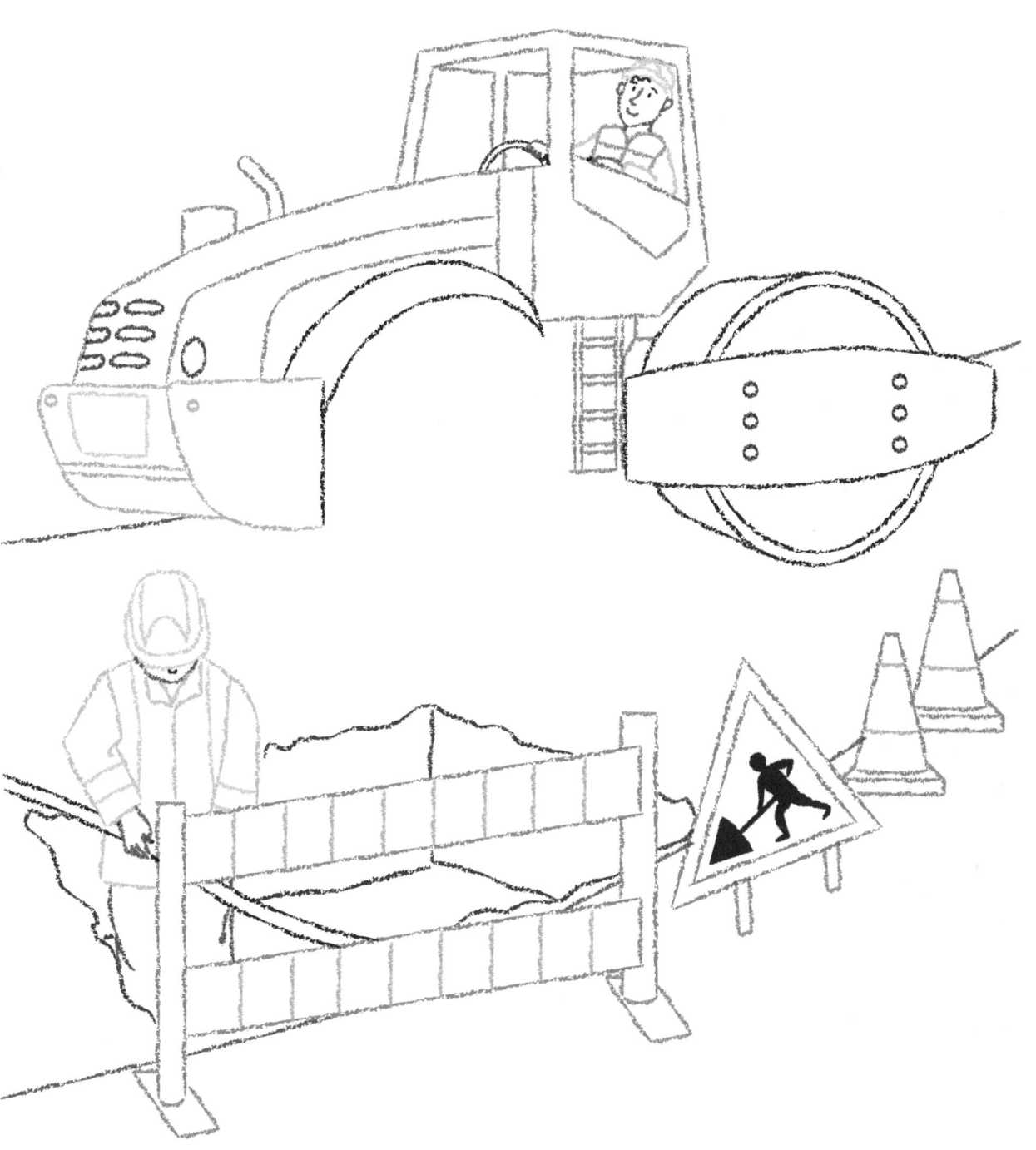

Sometimes old buildings need to be torn down. Put these demolition images in the correct order from start to finish.

Follow the line to see which building this wrecking ball is headed toward!

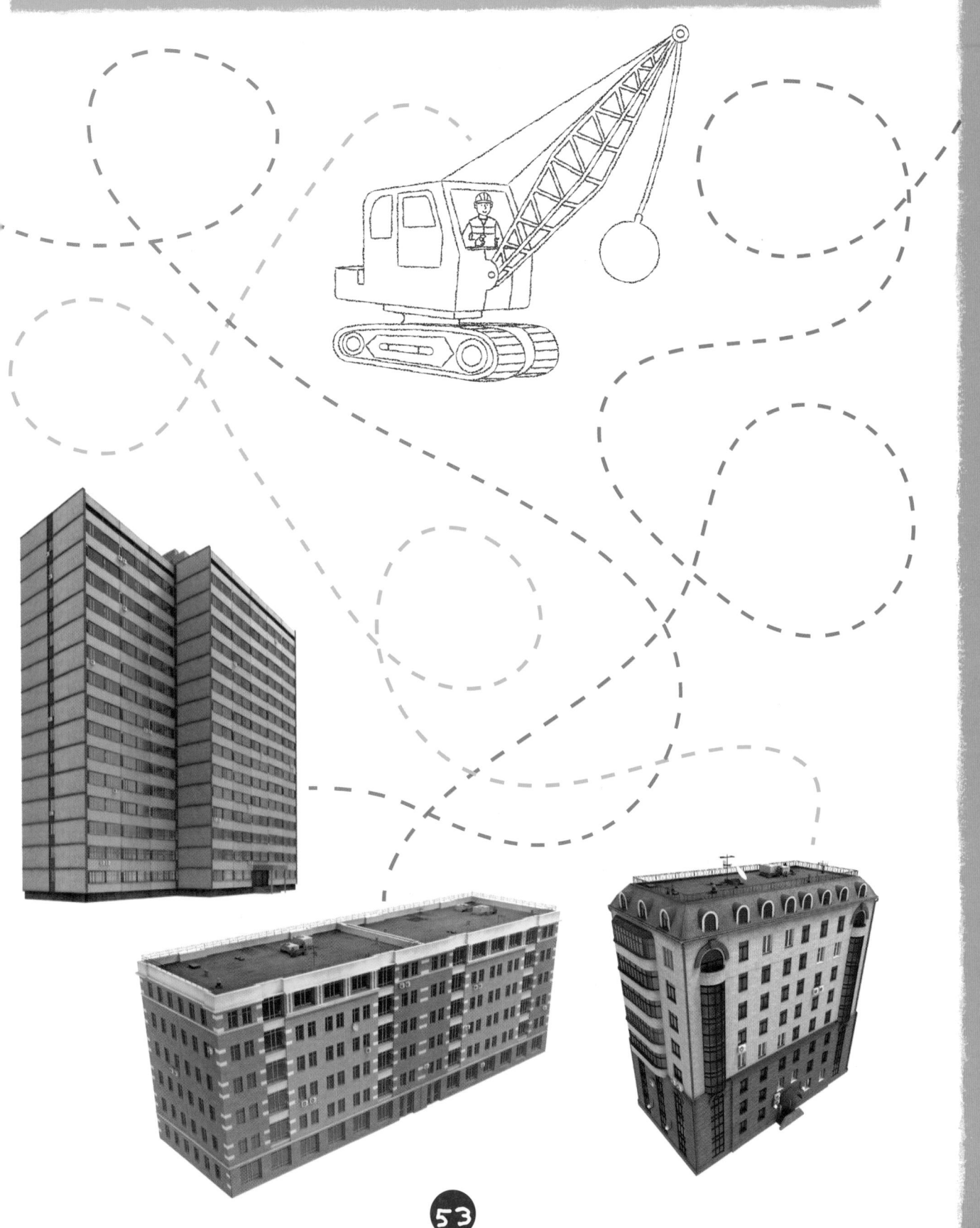

Find and circle the construction vehicles. Can you name them all?

Find the 5 differences between these toolboxes and then color them in.

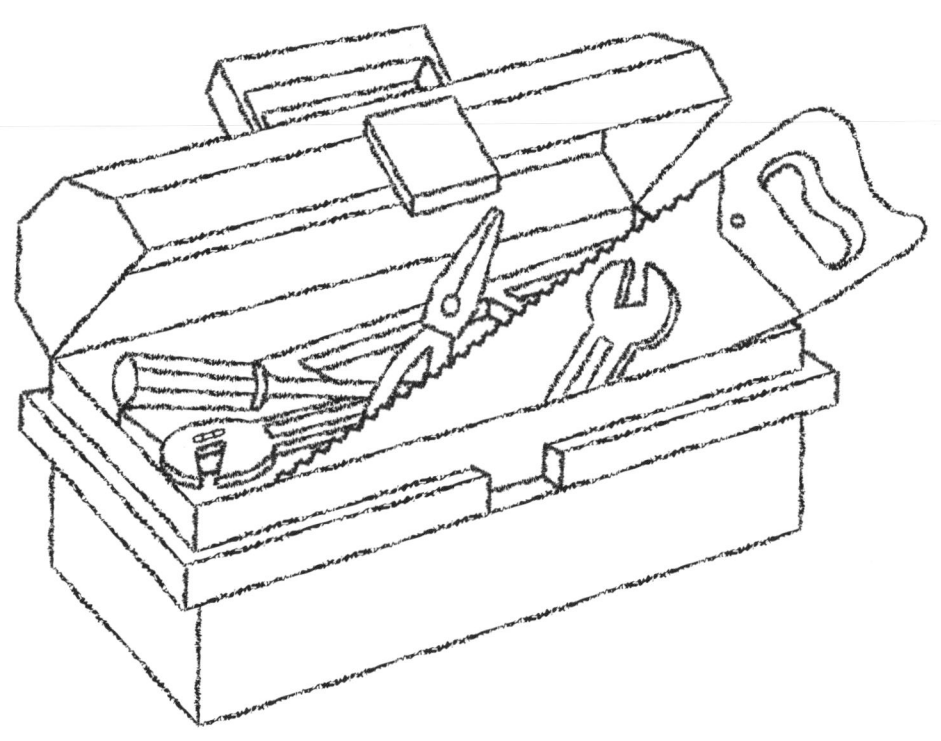

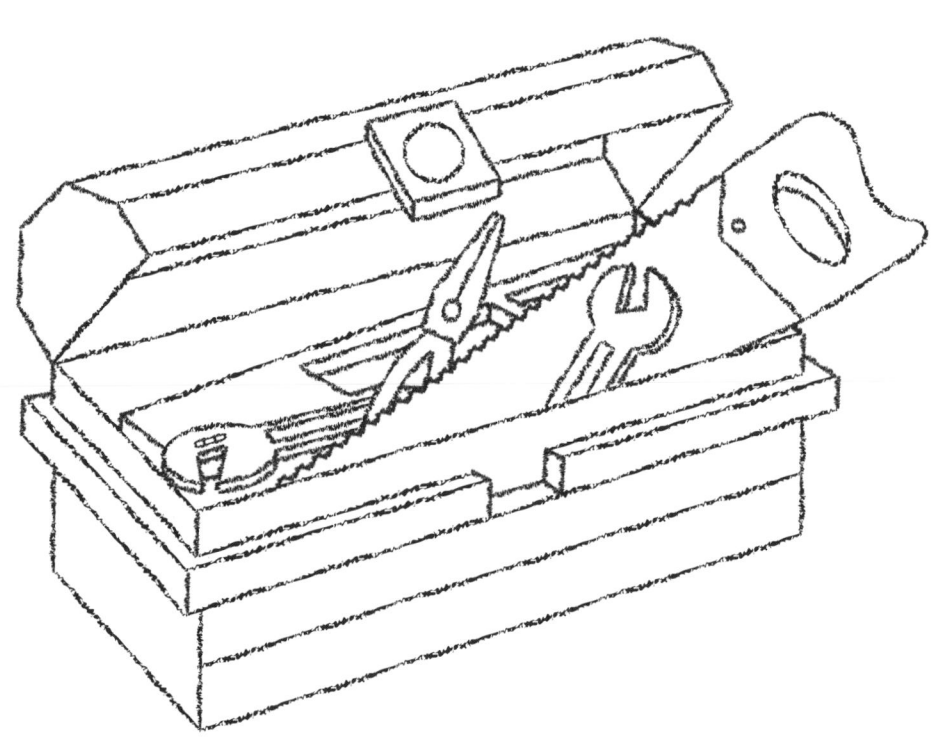

The carpenter is laying a new floor,
but some pieces of flooring are missing.
Can you find them on the sticker pages
and install them for him?

Find the two diggers that are the same and circle them.

Use your drawing skills to complete this house and color it in. Add some stickers for the final touch.

Find the materials on the sticker
pages that make each of these
finished items.

roof

roof tiles

tar

road

door

wood

stone

floor tiles

wall

bricks

It's break time! Which one of these construction workers gets to the coffee and cookies first?

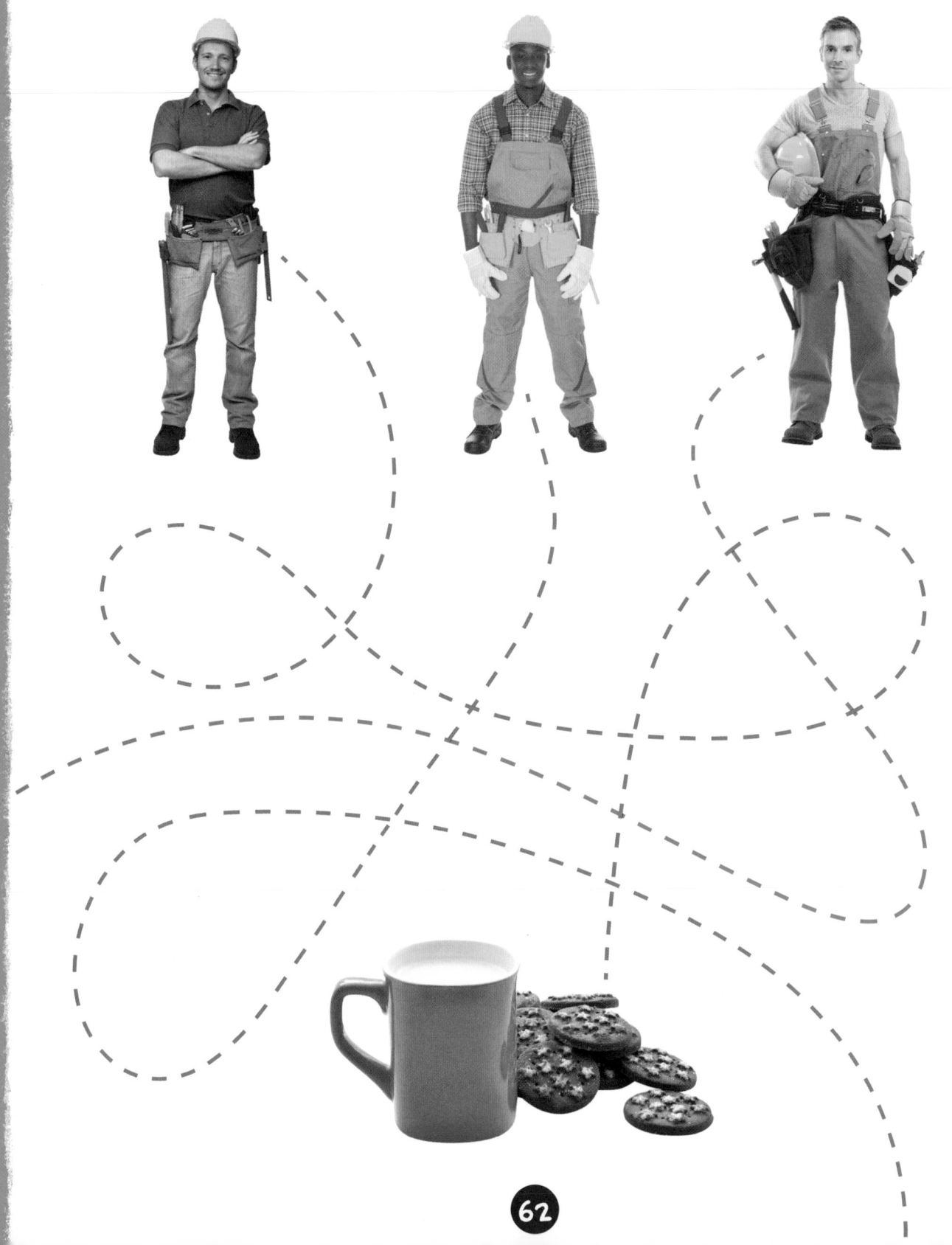

Can you find the machine that looks different from the others?

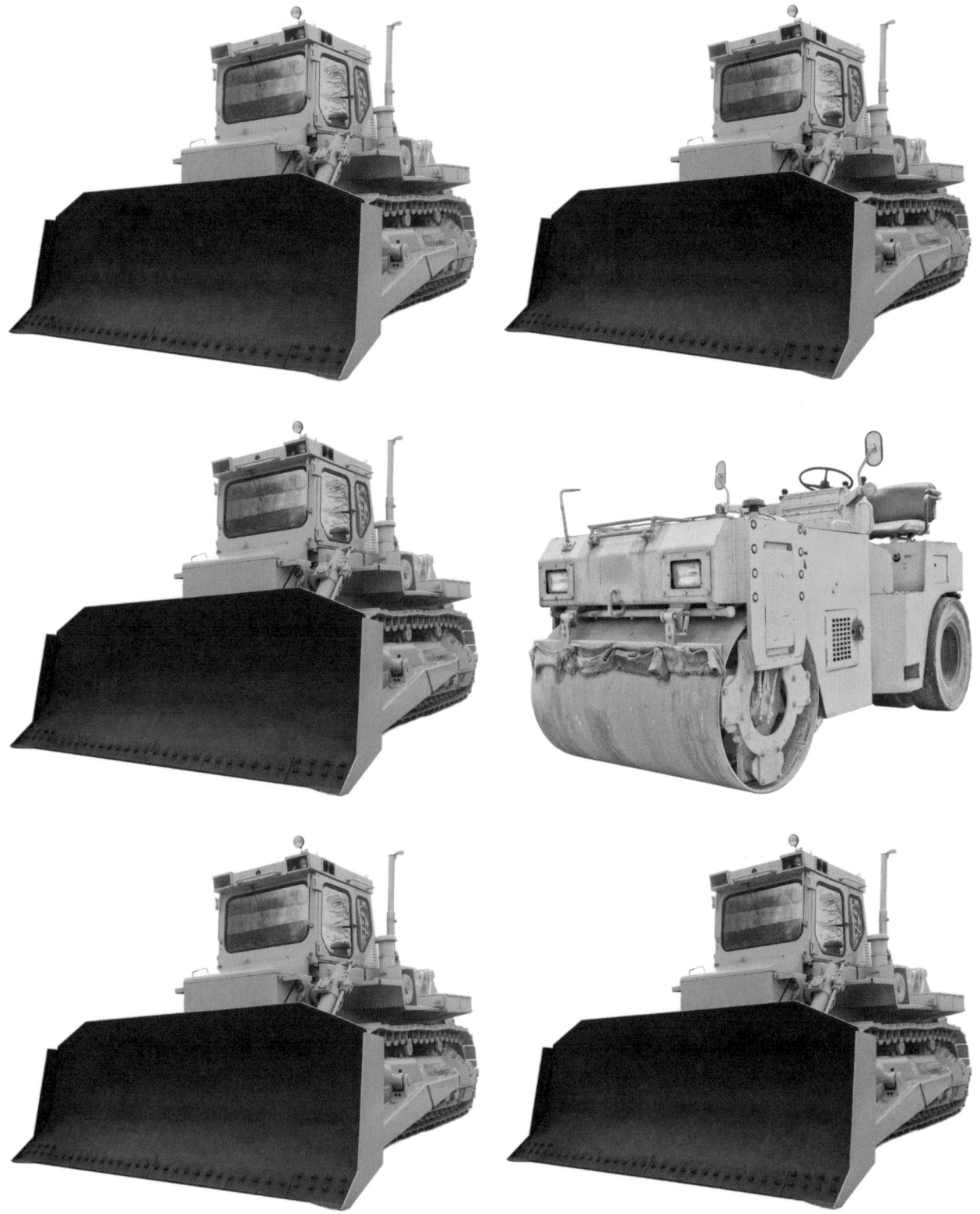

Color in this construction site.

A painter uses paint and other decorations to change the colors of walls. Can you find his missing tools on the sticker pages?

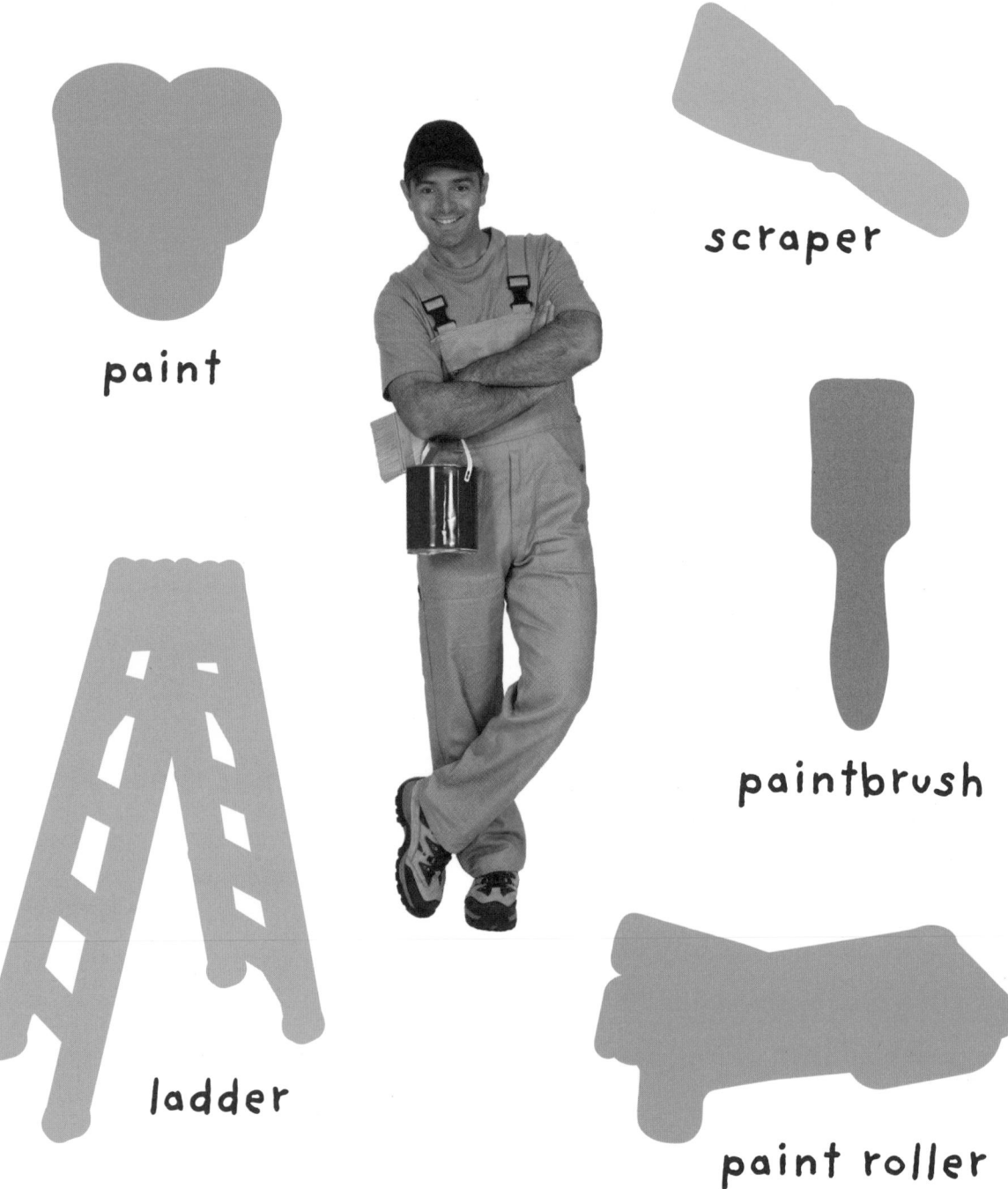

scraper

paint

paintbrush

ladder

paint roller and tray

Can you help this construction worker collect all the bricks and add them to the pile?

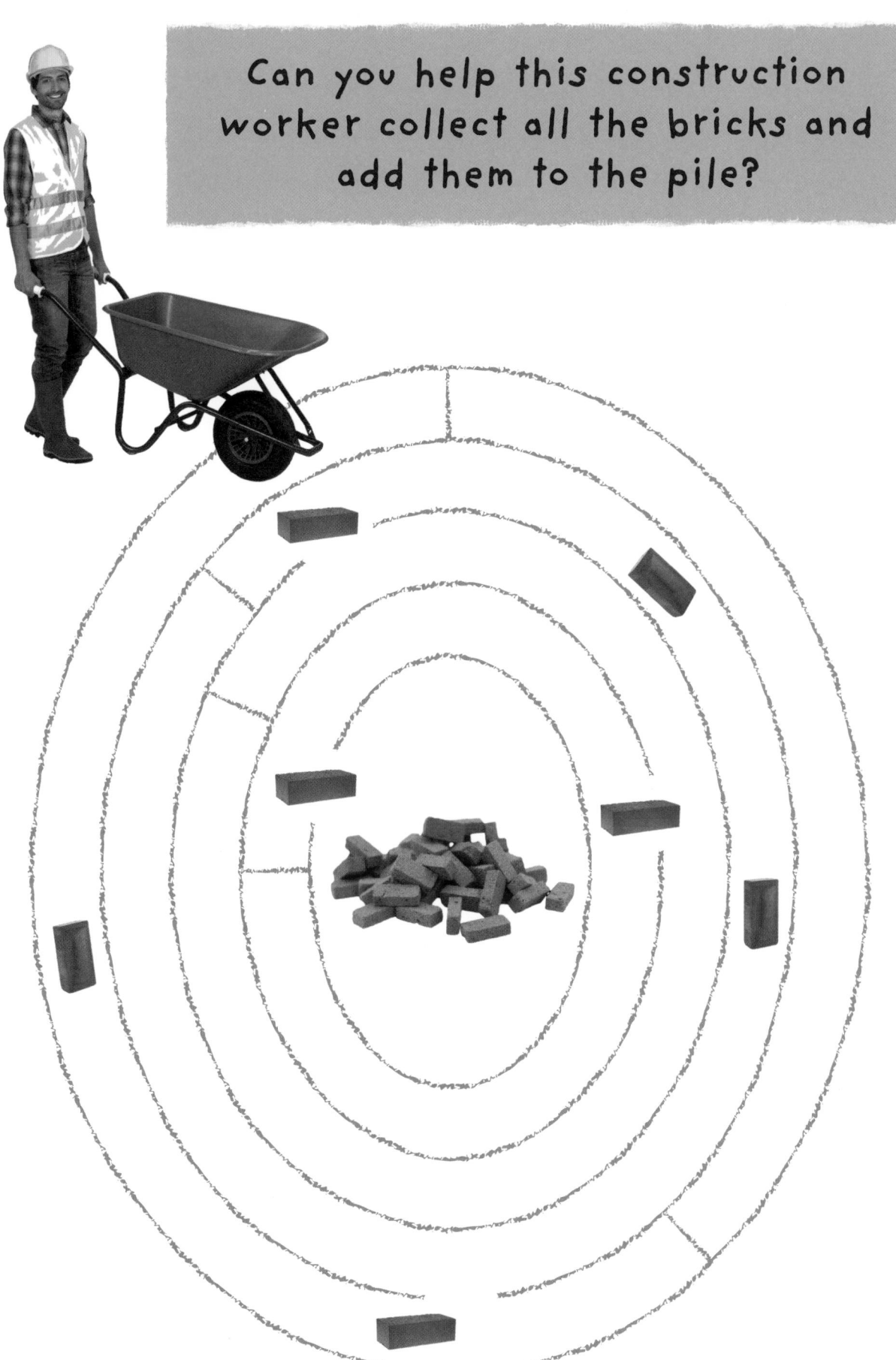

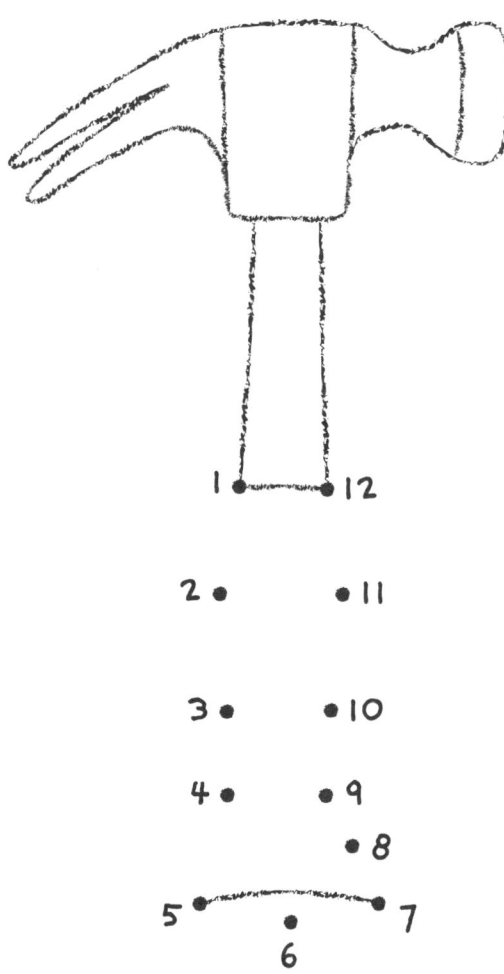

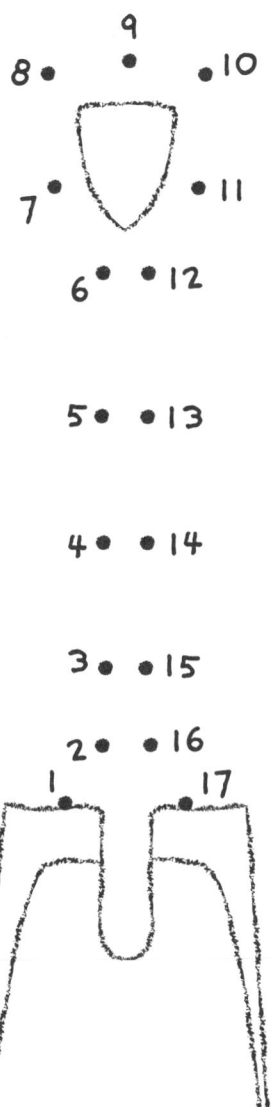

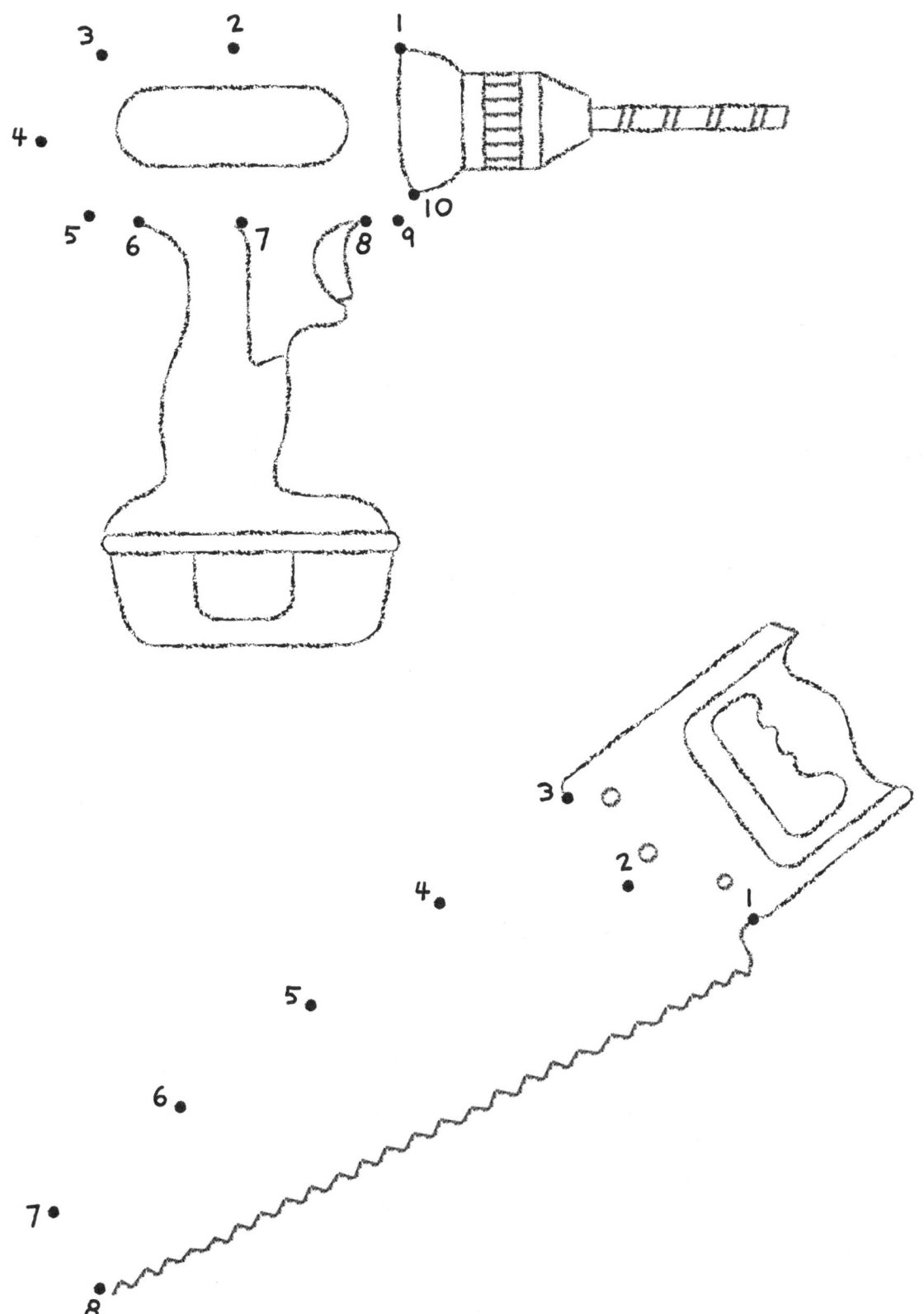

These vehicles can't go anywhere without their wheels! Can you find them on the sticker pages?

Building a house takes a long time!
Number these construction images from
1 to 4 to see how a house is built.

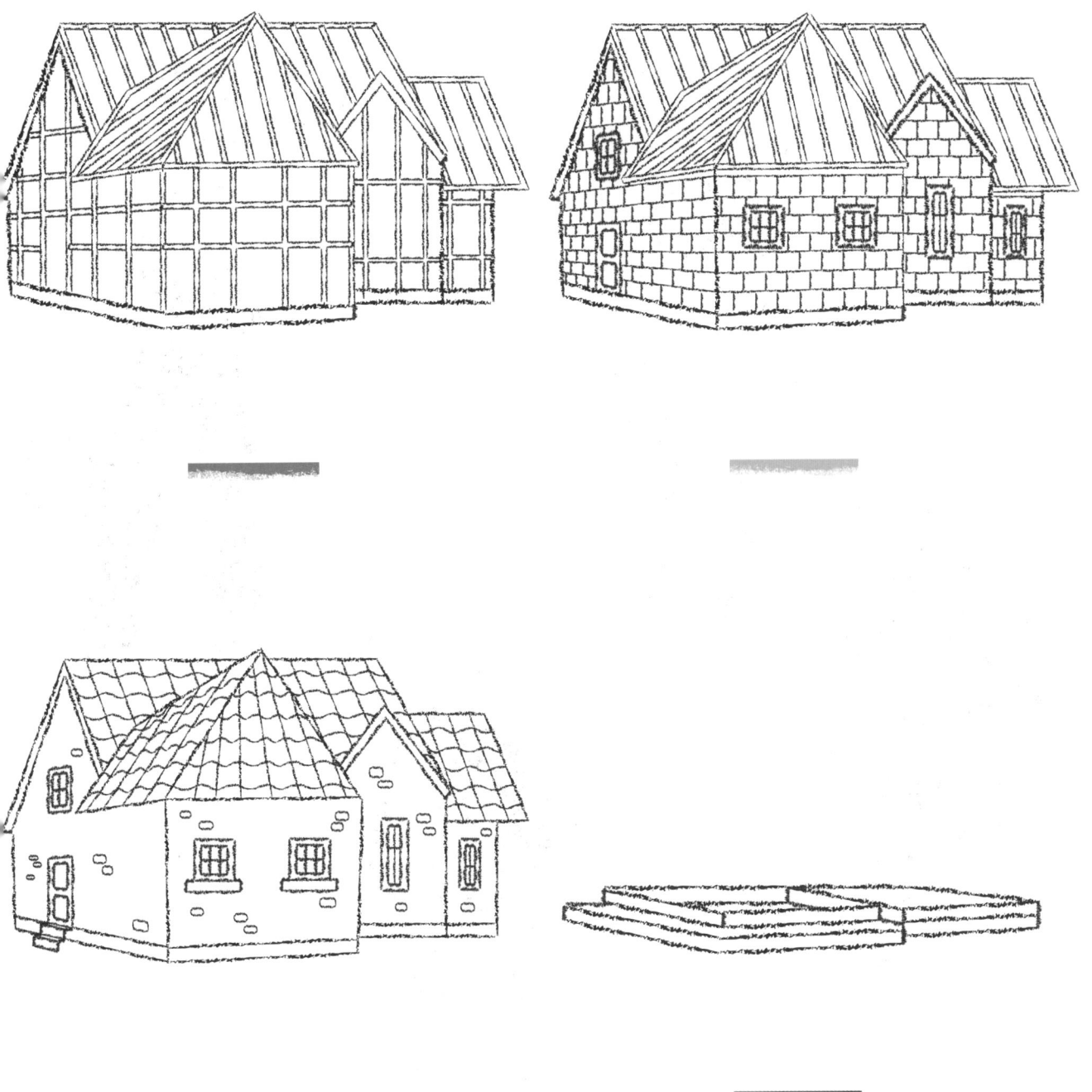

Some construction workers are called if there is an emergency. Match each construction worker to his or her emergency call.

Copy this dump truck on the blank squares and color it in.

Don't forget to draw what it's carrying!

Match each construction vehicle to its silhouette.

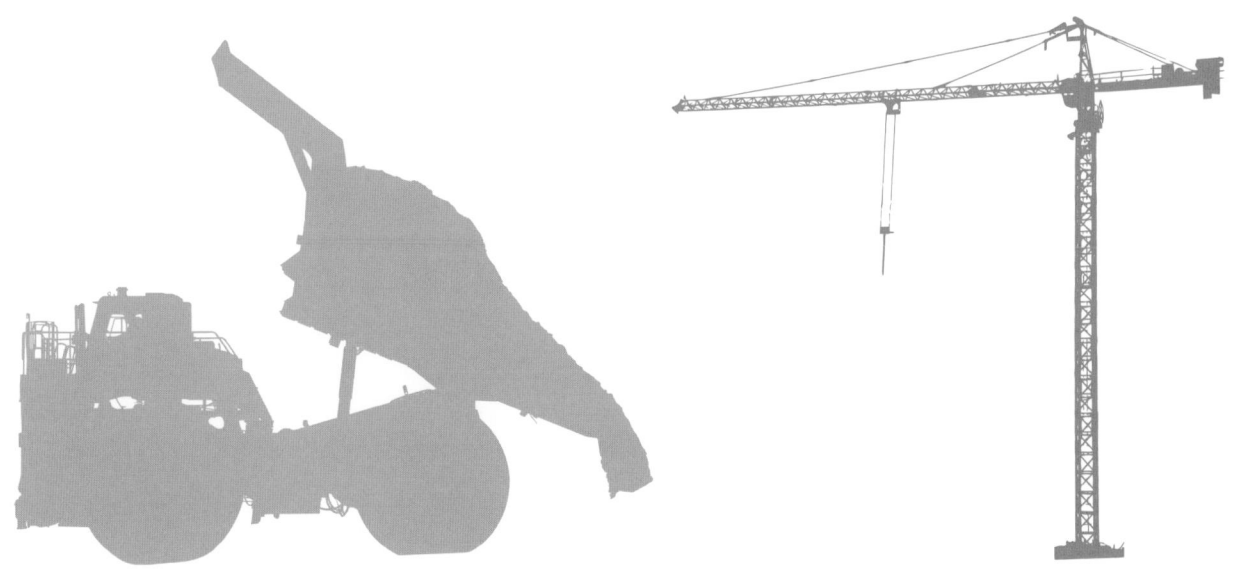

ANSWERS

Page 5:
Dump truck

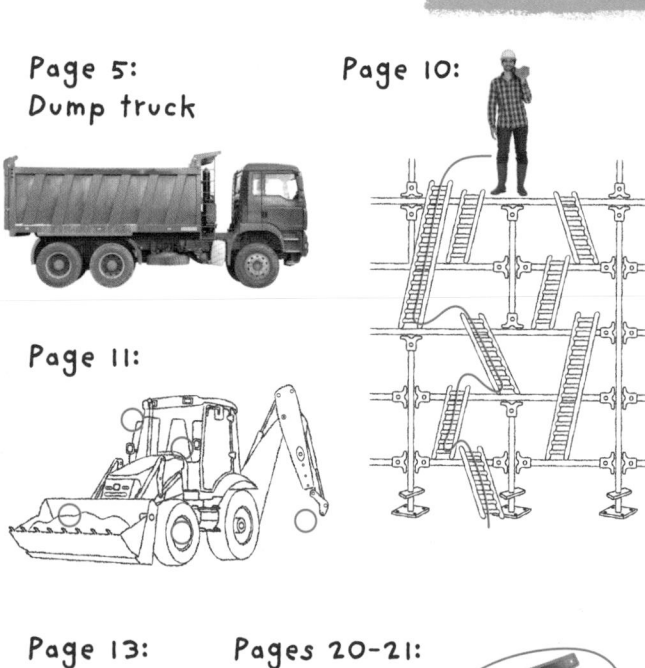

Page 10:

Page 11:

Page 13:

Pages 20-21:

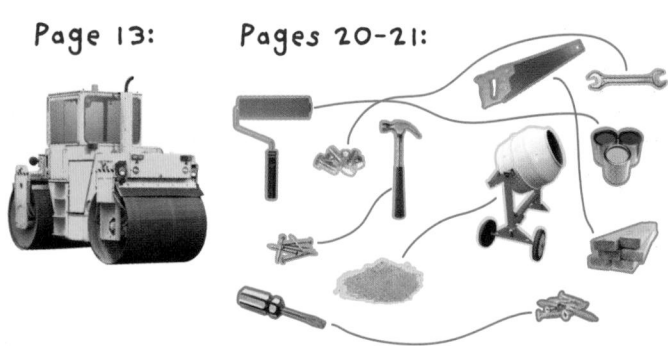

Page 22:

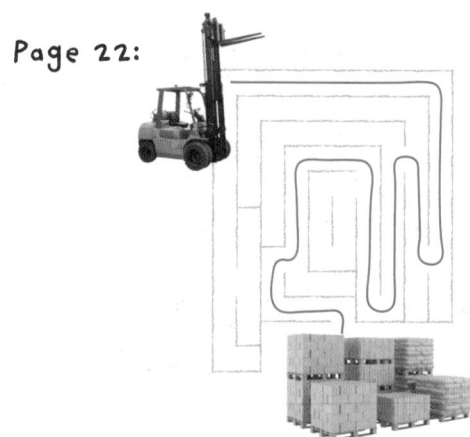

Pages 26-27:

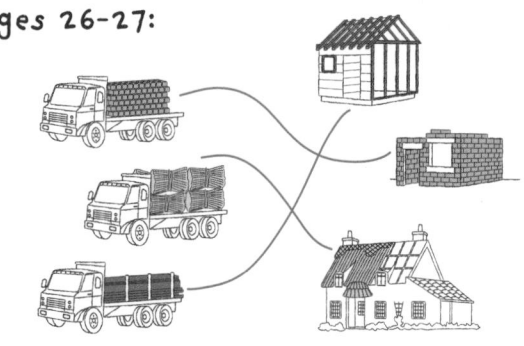

Page 28:
Toy bricks

Page 31:

Pages 32-33:

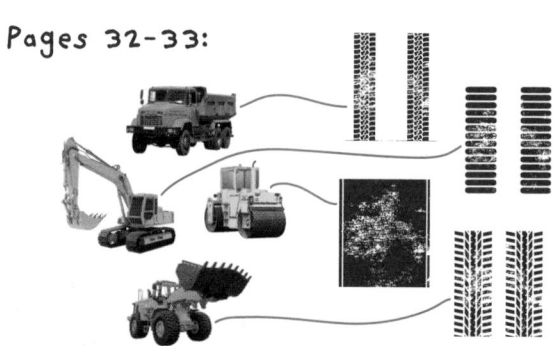

Page 34:

Page 36:

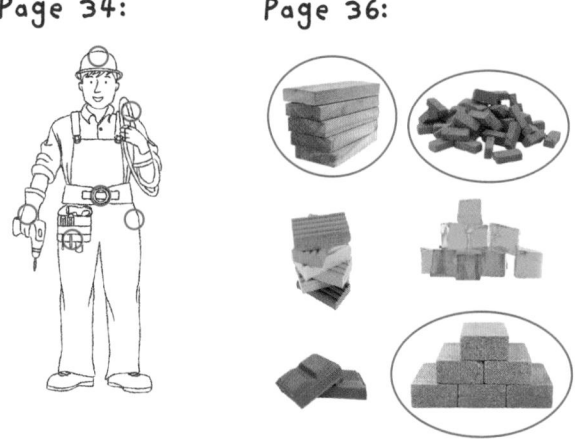

Pages 38-39:

ANSWERS

Page 40:

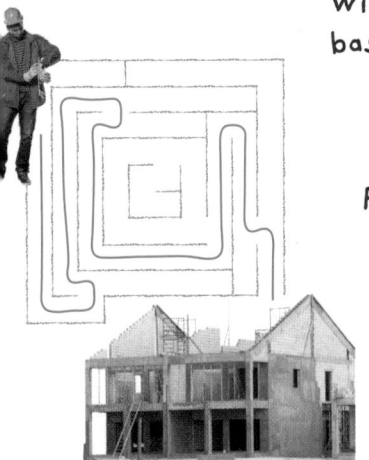

Page 41:
Wicker basket

Page 42:

Pages 44-45:

Page 46:
Hammer
Trowel
Screwdriver
Saw
Electric drill
Shovel

Page 52:

4   1

2   3

Page 50:

Pages 54-55:

Page 56:

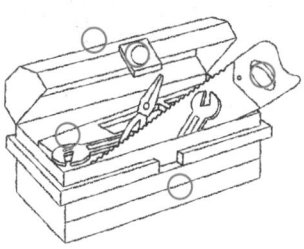

Page 58:

Page 63:
Steamroller

Page 67:

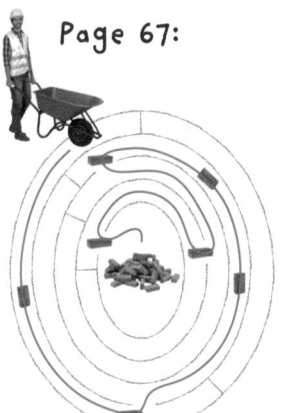

Page 71:

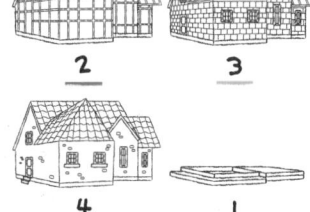

2   3

4   1

Pages 72-73:

Pages 76-77:

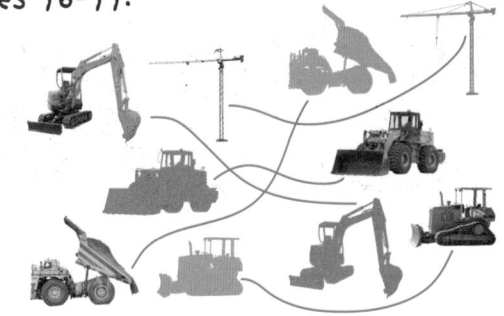

Good-bye,
construction site!

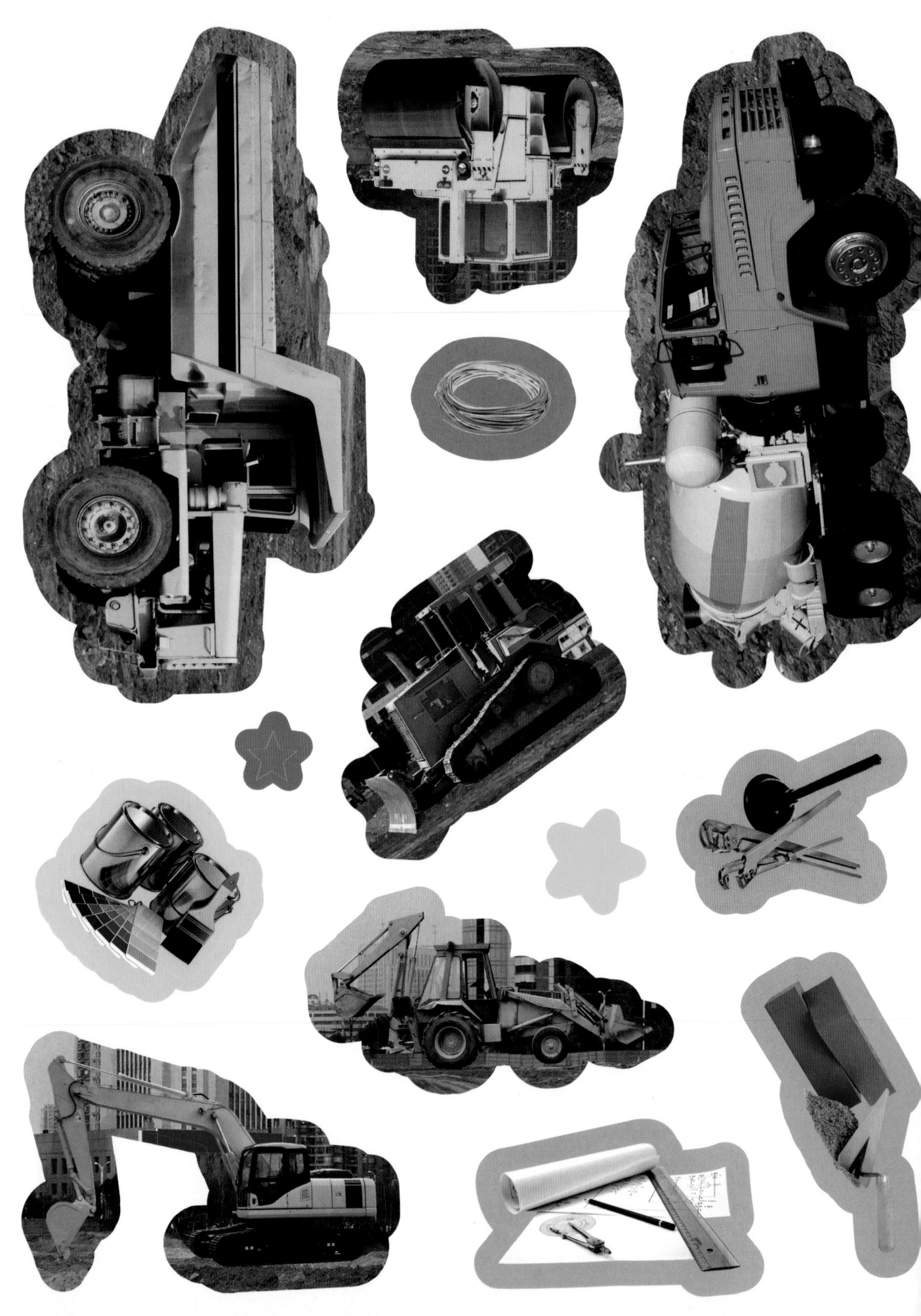